P9-DMQ-983

In Lucia's Eyes

In Lucia's Eyes

ARTHUR JAPIN

Translated from the Dutch by David Colmer

ALFRED A. KNOPF NEW YORK 2005

THIS IS A BORZOI BOOK
PUBLISHED BY ALFRED A. KNOPF

Translation copyright © 2005 by David Colmer

All rights reserved. Published in the United States by Alfred A. Knopf,
a division of Random House, Inc., New York, and in Canada
by Random House of Canada Limited, Toronto.

www.aaknopf.com

Originally published in Holland as *Een Schitterend Gebrek* by Uitgeverij De
Arbeiderspers, Amsterdam, in 2003. Copyright © 2003 by Arthur Japin.

Knopf, Borzoi Books, and the colophon are registered trademarks of
Random House, Inc.

Library of Congress Cataloging-in-Publication Data
Japin, Arthur, [date]
    [Schitterend gebrek. English]
    In Lucia's eyes / Arthur Japin ; translated from the
    Dutch by David Colmer.
      p. cm.
    ISBN 1-4000-4464-2
    I. Colmer, David, [date]   II. Title.
PT5881.2.A59S3513   2005
839.31'364—dc22   2005044316

Manufactured in the United States of America
First American Edition

for Elsa

Many things that exist only in the imagination later become real.

—G. C.

Contents

I

The Benefit of Love

If there's one thing I'm good at, it is love. That might not seem much, but I'm proud of it. I learned it the way a stray dog learns to swim: by being stuffed in a gunnysack with the rest of the litter and thrown into a fast-flowing river.

The one that survived against the odds, that's me. With the yelps of the drowned still ringing in my ears, I had to learn to love.

I didn't go under.

I made it to the other side.

Others carry a sorrow in their hearts. Unseen, it hollows them out from within. My salvation was that I wear my sorrow on the outside, where no one can miss it.

I

THE EVENING on which I came to see everything in a new light, I was planning to dine, as I did every Thursday, with Mr. Jamieson, a wholesaler of skins and tobacco, and then perhaps to go dancing with him. It was only after an attack of gout had forced the good merchant to cancel our appointment that I decided to visit my box at the theater.

Don't misunderstand me. I am not used to luxury. Since the calamity, I have been at life's mercy and am very frugal. I've had to be. For a long time I had no idea what the next day would bring: whether I would go hungry, whether anyone would shelter me, whether I would be attacked and forced to move on. Even after I'd finally attained a certain status in Amsterdam, I always limited myself to a bare minimum of finery—only what was expected in the circles I was obliged to move in and the sundries I needed to practice my profession. I never allowed myself extravagance. Nor did I feel the want of any. In the last couple of years, however, I did allow myself one thing: a permanent box seat at the French theater on the Overtoom, which I visited whenever time permitted.

I was on my way there that evening in mid-October. As usual, I had hired a small but respectable boat. There was a chill in the air. In Amsterdam the cold on the canals is worse than in

Venice. More piercing and insidious, it sets in months earlier and tends to settle in the bones rather than the lungs. All the same, I prefer a boat to a carriage. The people on the quays tend to ignore those who pass them on the water. More or less unnoticed, I am able to study others at my leisure. On the evening in question I was doing just that, partly for my own amusement and partly for professional reasons.

In the curve of the Herengracht, two gentlemen caught my eye. One of them I already knew: Jan Rijgerbos, a stockbroker. A friendly, cultivated widower, Rijgerbos is fit, well built, and undemanding. His companion was unknown to me. He had a dark complexion and a striking profile. It was the latter feature that immediately attracted my attention. His appearance touched me in a way I could not explain. I asked the boatman to row faster so that we might stay abreast of the two men walking on the quay, and I continued to study the stranger. His face was oval, and a blond wig framed it to advantage. Although not particularly handsome, he soon aroused my desire quite unexpectedly.

This annoyed me.

I am the one who arouses desire.

He was too slight for me anyway, I decided. What's more, dressed as he was according to the latest Paris fashion—in breeches of yellow silk that showed his calves—he cut an absurd figure in such bleak weather. I lost interest and began surveying the other pedestrians. As we passed under the Leidsebrug, however, Rijgerbos and his friend were just crossing it and I managed to catch a snatch of their conversation. They were speaking French: one with difficulty, the other with apparent ease. I liked the sound of the Frenchman's voice and ordered the boatman to stop beneath the arches of the bridge. We waited there in the shadows until the two men were out of sight.

· · ·

WERE IT NOT for the recklessly low neckline I was wearing, or that my thoughts that evening were far from elevated, or that I am scarcely the kind of woman a higher power would squander ten minutes of thought on—were it not for any of these incontrovertible facts, you might imagine that God, or maybe the devil, had arranged the whole thing for His entertainment. A coincidence like this! How rare it is that we are allowed a glimpse of the grand scheme within which all our lives are arranged. All the years of being buffeted by fate had not prepared me for what would follow. All that time I had been constantly on guard. And now, just as I was beginning to think that fortune had finally grown bored with tossing me about, it rose up again, coming to feral attention to seize me by the throat.

This time I cannot but accept that some catastrophes do have a purpose. It *does* make sense to persevere. I have been furnished with proof of that. Or at least, God willing, I soon will be.

I TOOK MY SEAT as usual shortly after the performance had begun, so as to offend as few spectators as possible. The opera was an old pastoral play that had recently been put to music by a composer from Grenoble. The performers were mainly the theater's regular company, and ovations welcomed the favorites. The lead, a shepherdess, was being played by a soprano who had triumphed in this role all over Europe.

Midway through the first act, Jan Rijgerbos knocked at the door of my box.

"Well, this is a surprise," I said. "I had no idea you liked the theater. I don't recall ever seeing you here before."

He was too well bred to show his discomfort at talking to me, but he did take care to remain out of sight of the audience below. I am used to that—no harm—and I didn't hold it against him.

"I must confess that the music is too mannered to my ear, but what do I know of it? No, I have a guest, a friend from France. He is visiting our city as an agent of the French treasury and insists on attending the theater every evening, as he does in Paris."

Rijgerbos stepped aside to reveal his guest, whom he introduced as Monsieur le Chevalier de Seingalt.

"They sold us our seats in the pit with the assurance that we'd have the best view of the performance," the man said in French, bowing to kiss my hand. "But no one warned us that the evening's most beguiling spectacle would not be onstage."

There is nothing a man can say to a woman that I haven't heard before. Compliments about appearance in particular always depress me, especially on a first meeting. From the outset, their sense of obligation seems to weary them. Dispatched on a mission they have no faith in, they inevitably stumble, like plow horses pressed to perform dressage, and their fatigue in the face of the task is evident from the outset. Some women live for sweet talk. I would rather go without. But how is a man to know that? Most aim to please with little understanding of our pleasure.

I cordially invited the gentlemen to join me in the box. Jan concealed himself behind the curtain, but Seingalt stepped forward unembarrassed in full view of everyone below. The yellow silk of his conspicuous suit seemed to light up in the glow of the downstage candles.

It was only when he was sure all eyes were upon us that he sat down and deliberately slid his chair closer to mine. This could mean only one of two things: Either Jan had told him nothing about me, or he had told him everything and Monsieur le Chevalier was an absolute fire-eater. Either way, I decided to like him.

We listened to the rest of the aria in silence, I all the while aware of Seingalt looking at me. He was trying to make out the outline of my face through the lace I was wearing as a veil. Although I knew he would not succeed, his attempt disturbed me. I had to master my breathing to avoid betraying my excitement. His eyes, large and black under heavy lids, would wander, sometimes down over my body, sometimes up in the hope of catching my expression.

When the big chandeliers were lit for the interval, I moved aside into the shadows. The chevalier began to inform me of his recent arrival from Paris and of his mission to ease France's beleaguered financial position by selling to the Dutch French government bonds that had depreciated because of the war. He was staying at the Star of the East, on the corner of the Nes and the Kuipersteeg. When he said this, he probed once more for an expression on my face, to no avail. Eventually he asked what no one in his position had dared to ask before: whether I would reward his friendly curiosity by allowing him a glimpse of my countenance. He was clearly unused to a woman's refusing him anything, because later he tried again, less politely. Finally he asked forthrightly why I would begrudge him something for which his desire had only deepened as we spoke.

"If you owned a valuable gem," I said, "you wouldn't oblige everyone who asked to gawk at it, would you?"

He smiled, conceding. "No, I would keep it in perfect safety."

"That is just how I keep myself, monsieur."

FROM THE DAY I first decided to wear a veil, I have found its effect on men to be remarkable. More than anything, men want that which has been withheld. A happy certainty is no match for a mystery denied. Given a choice, a man will always take the unknown.

"THIS GEM OF YOURS must be unique in the world," the savior of France remarked with a pout, letting his gaze glide mischievously down my bare throat, "considering that you have no qualms about exposing other treasures to the idle gawker."

"Give up, sir," I advised. "You have met your match."

I toyed with him a little longer until he fell silent and pretended that the singers, who had returned to the stage, were demanding his attention. Not to dash his hopes entirely, I opened my fan and laid it on the plush before him, a sign well understood all over Europe.

FOR YEARS I was accustomed to seeing myself in the eyes of others. I judged myself by their reactions to me. The looks they gave me were the key to who I was. Then I hit upon the idea of drawing a curtain over all that.

At first I covered my face only to go out. Constraining myself in this fashion, I found a freedom I could remember only from my earliest childhood. Since putting on the veil, I have lived as if reborn. Unseen by others, I have no need to look at myself. Delivered from the image that had eclipsed my every other sense of reality, I move once again through a world without danger, like a child among protective elders. They allow me more latitude, no longer seeing me as one of them. I don't have to join in their serious discussions. While they sit at table, I imagine myself crawling around on the floor between their legs. Children are aware of the judgment of adults but don't let it weigh on them. That is the lightheartedness I rediscovered in my disguise. And it pleased me so much that in the last few years I have drawn my veil over almost all my waking hours, even at home, sometimes even alone. At work I always wrap myself in it. It's what has made me so successful.

THE PLAY takes a dramatic turn. The squire warns the shepherdess: His son may be in love with her, but he will be disinherited if they marry. To preserve her beloved's happiness, she pretends to love another, then abandons her flock to join a convent. Just after she has become a bride of Christ, the lovesick youth comes knocking at the gate. He has discovered the whole scheme, but too late. She allows him one last look at her beauty. Then she dons the wimple and is lost to him forever.

"What desecration!" Seingalt sighed, as the soprano disappeared under her habit. His indignation was genuine and the words just slipped out. "Hiding something so beautiful; that must surely count as a mortal sin!"

"I am happy to leave the judgment of our sins to Him who invented them, monsieur."

He looked at me with a wry smile. "Perhaps He would take the same opportunity to explain why someone like you would choose to hide herself."

Soon after, I closed my fan and put it away. Heroines who sacrifice themselves needlessly should not count on my sympathy. I'm annoyed by silly geese who let their minds overrule their emotions, and glad to see them get what they deserve. Rather than sit through the rest of the act, I asked the gentlemen to excuse me. The pastoral was upsetting, and I come to the opera to be diverted, not disturbed.

In Lucia's Eyes

. . .

IT WAS HARDLY the first time I had been accused of hiding behind my veil. A frequent misconception, since quite the opposite is true.

I hide the world.

I have lowered a curtain before it.

Through that haze of lace and silk it looks so much softer.

2

I DON'T REMEMBER any boundaries. Pasiano, the estate where I was born, extended out over the hills as far as the eye could see. The doors were always open. I could walk for hours and, whichever way I went, everything was familiar. My parents never worried about me. In the morning, when I raced off after a bird or a rabbit, they weren't afraid to see me disappear. They knew that by midday the smells spreading out over the fields from the kitchens would lure me home for lunch. While still young I befriended the horses in the meadows, and in time they let me ride them, with my hands clinging to their manes and my heels in their flanks. The chicks from the fowl yard were my toys, and the overseer's dogs were my playmates. Together we rolled down the golden slopes and ran through the woods. The streams in the valleys were warm and shallow, and until my tenth birthday the gamekeepers were forbidden to set traps. At Pasiano there was no danger. There were no limits to my happiness. I spent my childhood fearless and unjudged.

I had no reason to believe that things in the world beyond its grounds were any different.

Like everyone else, I learned to feel before I learned to think. It was only after people had begun to teach me that I began to distinguish things and recognize facts. But I never put what I was taught above the things I knew intuitively. Even now, I am reluctant to admit disagreeable realities. Self-delusion has the benefit of letting us believe that everything is still possible. I have a talent for that. It makes me feel less afraid. Were the devil staring me straight in the face, I would still convince myself that my visitor was an angel. I'm sure I could even set Lucifer to doubting.

I believe in dreams. I understand them, feel at home in them. For my first fourteen years, I lived one. That doesn't mean I won't see the truth. I actually see it much too clearly. Sometimes I screw up my eyes to shut out the glare of reality, so I can feel secure a little longer, even when the smell of sulfur is already burning in my nose.

Those first few years I thought Pasiano was ours—from the grain fields of Squazaré, where the sun rises, to Rivarotta, where the storks settle down in November to winter; from the deer wood near Codopé up to Azanello, where the sun disappears at night behind the ruined castle of the Montefeltros. I simply had no reason to think that my world did not belong to me.

In reality, the estate was the property of the Countess of Montereale, who for reasons of health spent the summer months there. She had a husband, Count Antonio, whom she loved with great tenderness, though he lived in Milan with his mistress. The countess had a daughter too, but she—Adriana—was seldom to be seen, since the countess hoped to establish her in the beau monde of Venice, where she lived under the watch of her tutor, a Frenchman called Monsieur de Pompignac.

Compared with the wealth of most noble families, the Montereales' fortune was modest. Without unremitting attention and years of careful planning, Adriana would not have stood the slightest chance in the matrimonial market. The competition in the upper echelons of Venetian society was murderously keen. To attain a position, a girl had to shine at all the big parties, not just during the season but in summer as well: at the country homes on the Brenta and at the most important summer residences elsewhere in the Veneto.

Without her daughter to keep her company, the countess was lonely at Pasiano and full of unspent affection. She directed it to me. She was used to having me around and liked it when I played in the drawing room. Even when she had guests, she would look out through the French doors, and if she saw me in the meadow she would call me in and take me on her lap. I called her auntie and believed she was part of our family.

One day in spring, one of her cousins came to stay. He was fleeing an outbreak of the smallpox in Chioggia and had brought his young son with him. Like me, the boy was six years old, and we became friends. I showed him my paradise, but he didn't seem to see it. I picked out a downy chick from the fowl yard and gave it to him as a gift, but he shrugged and let it go. Near the rapids, I showed him how you could catch the dragonflies that danced in the spray without hurting them. Fascinated, he accepted the insect I offered him and declaring that he intended to become a surgeon, he then broke the creature's wings so that he could practice tying on splints. Later, the boy climbed onto one of the dogs, and when he tried to spur the animal with his heels, naturally it bit him. To me that seemed only fair. The dog hadn't even drawn blood, but the boy made a big show of it. He ran to his father, who demanded that the overseer put down his animals that same day. We watched as they were gathered into gunnysacks. As I sobbed, inconsolable, the countess pulled me over to the couch and, as if fearing she might lose me too, held me tight and rocked me soothingly.

"You see, my dear," she whispered. "You see what happens when you let someone get too close to the things you love."

Soon after, the boy left for Gemona with his father, who announced that the pox had not reached those regions. In reality, the countess had asked her cousin to leave. He blamed me for that and, climbing into the coach, exclaimed spitefully that it was irresponsible to allow a highborn child to play with the daughter of a kitchen maid.

That evening my mother revealed the difference between servants and nobles. She explained that the countess was not really my aunt and that we had no say over what happened on the estate. We lived there at her sufferance, dependent on her kindness.

This weighty revelation made no difference to my own life at Pasiano. I was as ever free in the fields and woods and still had the run of the manor. It was no less precious to me. The Countess of Montereale continued to shower me with love. Still, a sorrow had been born. It wasn't something I imagined. All the next summer it shimmered in the wheat, and that winter I heard it in the honking of the geese.

Few can fathom the power of a word. Just one, spoken thoughtlessly, can change the world. Truth is more than the things you see; that is why its value is only relative. I am very careful with it.

MY MOTHER WASN'T a common maid. She and my father ran the household, she herself being responsible for the domestic staff and the care of guests.

My father's family had been in the service of the Montereales for five generations when my mother visited the estate as a young girl in the winter of 1728. There was never any intention of her staying. At the time she was apprenticed to her father and had traveled with him to supervise the installation of the gigantic mirrors he had designed for the grand salon at

Pasiano. The heavy work was carried out by a few of the local foresters, who had been temporarily excused from their usual duties. My father was one of them. Despite the cold they took off their shirts and worked up such a sweat installing the works of art that the salon windows steamed over.

My grandfather's fame extended far beyond Venezia Giulia. His designs could be found from Vienna to Milan; even the great Tiepolo admired his work. He made his mirrors by a technique he had learned on journeys to Tiflis and Constantinople: Instead of cutting the front of the glass, he did his engraving on the back, in several layers under the mercury. His sumptuous designs created an illusion of extraordinary depth. There seemed to be another—intangible—dimension behind the glass. Dazzling and fey, it caught and reflected the light in ways the people in our region had never seen before. Season after season, it was fashionable to have one's house decorated by my grandfather. His glass frames embellished paintings, windows, and doors; his wealthy patrons tried to astonish their guests by having tables and even chairs blown from glass, just so that my grandfather could engrave them using his secret method. In those years, boudoirs and salons everywhere were filled with baubles he had decorated. His popularity reached its peak when he developed a method of applying copper powder and gold foil to the back of the glass, imbuing the mirror with a gentle glow, so that anyone looking into it would see a flattering image without blemishes or imperfections. The great families of Venice prized his work even above the glass of Murano, so to this day all who look into the mirrors of the Mocenigo, Venier, and Zorzi palaces see a gentler version of themselves framed by glittering apparitions drawn by my grandfather.

By the time I was born, the aristocracy had long since moved on to a new fashion. My grandfather's fame was a thing of the past, but that didn't pain him. Success had exhausted him. After years of working to order, he was happy to return to the fount of his inspiration, pleasing no one but himself, no longer a craftsman but now an artist. Few were those whose taste followed his muse's fancy, but some still occasionally sought him out for a commission, among them the Countess of Montereale. She had resolved to mark the birth of her daughter by refurbishing the ballroom at Pasiano.

The work took five full weeks.

It was during that time it happened.

"You had me in agonies," my mother would upbraid my father. "That divine glass in those coarse peasant hands! It's a miracle it wasn't shattered to bits. Entrusting something like that to you; I don't know what I was thinking!" Meanwhile, by the look in her eyes, he knew she was relishing the memory. "A clod like you handling something fragile and refined?" She often enacted tirades like this to provoke him into grabbing her by the waist with those big, coarse hands, just as he had done back then. She succeeded effortlessly. In no time he was lifting her up, producing shrieks of delight.

"Let go of me, you big oaf!" she would scream. "You're liable to break me too! You expect me to give myself to you? Like giving a crystal chalice full of honey to a bear!" As always during this theatrical interlude, my father would respond by roughly licking her face, as if it were covered with the sweetness of bees. My parents were not at all embarrassed by their behavior; in fact, the whole performance seemed designed to show me how fiercely the love that had created me still raged within them.

"I noticed that father of yours ogling me those first few days in the salon," my mother would say, when I was in love myself. It was the first and only time we would speak more as friends than as mother and daughter. I was fourteen. Her confidences made me uneasy, but I was glad to be taken seriously. No one had a keener understanding of love, so it pleased me when she realized that, young as I was, I had found mine.

"The slug, he never once looked straight at me," she told me, "but I kept catching his eye in the mirrors. At first I was flattered, but in a few days, when he was still circling and gawking, I got fed up. It was infuriating. I grew jealous of my own reflection. I waited until my father had left for lunch with the other workmen and asked him what he meant by staring so brazenly. He had to summon all his courage to answer. 'I wasn't looking at you,' he mumbled, even then speaking only to the glass, not me. 'It's your father's artistry,' he said, 'it's so mysterious and beguiling I can see my future in it.' I snorted contemptuously, never one for that kind of drivel, but it turned out he meant it. When he sensed I might be pleased, he grabbed my wrist painfully. 'I'm sorry,' he said, 'but I don't dare to avert my eyes from my good fortune any longer.' He refused to let go until I had seen what he was referring to. Heavy-handed, he forced me to look at myself. A glimpse wouldn't satisfy him, no, I had to stare into my own eyes. He was almost threatening. I was afraid he might have come from one of those Alpine peasant families inbred to the point of lunacy. The safest thing was to humor him. So I kept looking. It wasn't easy. Don't forget, I grew up in a workshop full of mirrors. No matter where I looked, I could always see myself. I thought I had a good idea of what I looked like, but now I saw something else. Not better or worse, but more complete. Suddenly I realized that I had never taken in more than my outline and had always avoided looking myself in the eye. I can't explain it any other way. Until then I had seen my likeness as if it were the work of some second-rate painter, studiously detailed but lifeless. Now, however, I saw myself as a great artist might capture his subject in a quick sketch, conveying with a few strokes the radiance that betrays a beating heart and warm, rapid breathing. Eventually the madman relaxed his grip. I looked at him. His eyes were filled with tears. 'It's all right,' I told him. 'I saw it.'"

My mother rocked me for a while, knowing it would be the last time. Finally, she kissed me, a sign that our intimate conversation was over, and spoke in a voice suddenly resolute and factual, as if to round off my entire upbringing. "That, darling, is the only thing that counts—for someone to see more in you than you ever imagined was there."

The young couple in the salon could scarcely conceal their transformation. As soon as my grandfather returned from his lunch break, he saw that he would have to let his daughter go. The radiant pair so pleased the Countess of Montereale that she refused to let them leave for Pordenone after the mirror room was completed, offering them an enviable position as the housekeepers of Pasiano.

THAT IS HOW I came to be born that same year, in an enormous four-poster bed in one of the second-floor guest rooms. On the day of my birth, my grandfather made a small round mirror. It hung above my cradle like a glittering toy. Facets cut into the edge refracted the light and sent the colors of the rainbow dancing over my bedclothes and the curtains of my cradle. That cherished object is the only possession I have held on to through everything. The decoration is simple: a garland of vines held aloft by four small cherubs. In the deepest layer of the glass, visible only in direct light, a dish has been engraved, and on it the eyes that are the symbol of the saint I was named for: Santa Lucia.

3

THE AUTUMN STORMS reached Holland early that year. In all my time in Amsterdam, I hadn't seen anything like it. Seven boats sank on the Zuider Zee. Two broke up in dock. Five souls were lost, buried alive when a house collapsed on the Keizersgracht, and God knows how many died in the Gardens, where an entire block was consumed by a fire that the wind kept raging for three whole days. To top it all, the spring tide breached the seawall. The dike guard repaired it that same night, but the series of disasters weighed heavily on the city.

On Friday there was a lull, though the threat was not yet over. Around half past three, we heard a town crier. He stood on the corner by the old men's home announcing that all chimneys out of plumb were to be pulled down immediately, as more gales were expected.

Giovanna and Danaë looked at me next to them in the mirror. We were just primping. The girls had been working hard all week, and having spent a lot of time indoors—the rooms I provide are comfortable but small—we all felt like a bit of air. The two girls, both from Parma, so much more agreeable, didn't know another soul in Amsterdam. They had set their hearts on going to a music hall. As the storm had confined all vessels to harbor and the city was overflowing with sailors and ships' captains, the two friends were keen to try their luck. I myself had been invited to dine with Jan Rijgerbos. His invitation had been friendly and most promising; I didn't want to disappoint him. And so we all ventured off, not that we were really in a position to do otherwise. Times were hard. I had used Spanish paper to apply a light blush over my protégées' white lead cheeks and chosen the correct beauty mark for each. Then I had laced their corsets and they mine. I put on a dress of deep-blue chintz. They chose a thinner fabric that accentuated their youthfulness, and we admired ourselves in the mirror. I felt strong and beautiful and was eager to preserve the feeling. For this evening I chose a purple veil, embroidered in Bruges by the nuns of Saint Anne's.

Jan called for me at home. To my surprise, he didn't take me to his residence on the Herengracht or to one of the establishments where he dared to be seen with me. Instead, we followed the Amstel to the family's country house at Ouderkerk. There we found a small group of friends sitting in front of the fire. I recognized two gentlemen: Rindert Bolhuys, the sexton of the South Church, with whom I had occasionally risked a jig, and my friend Jamieson, the merchant from Massachusetts. They were listening to a stranger telling a story. His back was turned to me, but I recognized his voice. It was the Frenchman from the opera. He was halfway through an account of the grisettes of Paris, young women who eke out a living by the sweat of their brow.

Jan noticed me flinch but held me firmly by the arm.

"What have you arranged?" I asked.

"Don't be so touchy. It's only a little entertainment."

"I like clarity. Your invitation did not mention any others. I was expecting our usual evening alone."

"Blame Jacques de Seingalt. He insisted on seeing you again."

At that the Frenchman noticed me. He concluded his story, saying that common girls such as he was describing were better off than ladies of breeding because they were able to live independently, free of the restraints of polite society. Instead of basking in the success of his tale, he abandoned his audience to come over and greet me.

"Have no illusions," Jan whispered. "He's already courting an alderman's daughter. Still, for days now, he hasn't stopped asking about you."

"What have you told him?"

"Everything," he said reassuringly, "except the truth."

WE DINED TOGETHER, then retired to the drawing room for some music. The gentlemen discussed financial matters and affairs of state. Mr. Jamieson was asked about the progress of the British war against the French and Indians in Canada. He called the conflict a blessing for New York, a city where he had recently acquired several warehouses and planned to settle in the near future.

"Money is streaming in from all sides," he said, "to pay and maintain the troops. For a merchant like me, who makes his fortune where it is to be made, these are golden times. In just a few years the harbor of New York has outgrown Boston's, and the streets are grander than Philadelphia's. There are twelve churches already and several hundred shops."

"Is it not true," asked Bolhuys bluntly, "that a lot of strange characters gravitate there, riffraff who wouldn't be tolerated anywhere else?"

"People from across the world do come to New York to try their luck, that's true. The restless atmosphere is ideal for anyone with some past he hopes to escape—"

"What married man hasn't one?" exclaimed Jan cheerfully.

"—and anyone who wants to reinvent himself."

"I have been told," announced Seingalt, who naturally took the side of the French, "that there are more slaves in your city than in the other northern states and that when they rose up they were quashed even more brutally than in the South. What, do you think, will be left of your prosperity if France triumphs and grants the Negroes their liberty?"

"That, monsieur, would be as catastrophic as a rain of glowing coals," Jamieson replied, "and just as likely."

After this, the men spent some time discussing the constant discord between the two nations. I tried to remain aloof and amuse myself with the other guests, but no one failed to notice that the two men were in complete disagreement about everything, whether it be Catholic confession, the consumption of raw fish, or the various uses of citrus fruit. The debate grew dangerously heated when Seingalt announced that he considered the influence of the Duke of Brunswick over the Dutch Crown Prince Willem a particular menace, owing to the former's preference for England over France. His words were so piqued and curt that I began to believe him jealous at having to share my attentions with Jamieson. After his outburst, the company thought it better to confine the conversation to pleasantries, and the other gentlemen began to jest about Seingalt's virility and conquests. He diverted attention from this subject with an account of the national lottery for the École Militaire, which he had established in concert with d'Alembert and Diderot. Then he told a long story of the attempted assassination of Louis XV, an event he claimed to have witnessed by virtue of his employment as a secret agent of the court. The chevalier thus revealed himself to be a man prone to getting completely carried away by his own tales.

When he had warmed everyone up, he set up a game with magic squares and pyramids. Radiating complete conviction, he ginned us up, presenting his scheme as the key to the interpretation of the cabala. Jan confided to me that Seingalt had performed the same parlor trick with great success at all the courts of Europe and had often met with the same unreserved credulity evident tonight. One would ask a question, the letters of which he would assign a numerical value. He then conjured with these numbers until answers appeared. The answers, too, had numerical correspondences of his own devising, even as he claimed to have no influence over the result. I must say he played his role so masterfully that one might easily have believed he was receiving messages from an oracle or power beyond himself. Several of those present were genuinely anxious to hear what the future had in store for them. Seingalt proposed to tell my future as well, but I declined the offer, explaining that I preferred to be guided by the past.

Around ten o'clock it became necessary to close the shutters. The trees were still in full leaf, though the recent storm had already uprooted several along the river. Now, with the wind rising again, there was a danger that others might fall as well. We were asked to leave the drawing room, which was, precariously, adjacent to the dike. Most of the company chose to return to the city, among them Mr. Jamieson, who offered to take me home. I declined this offer too, preferring, as I told him, to stay a little longer to listen to Seingalt.

"As you will," grumbled Jamieson, "but I'd watch that Frenchman. How can you trust a nation constantly devouring onions? It disturbs the sleep. No wonder there's not a man left in Paris who hasn't traded his dreams for a conviction."

Those who chose to remain spread out over the other rooms. The Chevalier de Seingalt ensconced himself with me in one of the antechambers. No one disturbed us there, and having enacted the customary civilities he set about his business.

I must admit, his technique revealed an impressive knowledge of the female soul. Now that we were alone, he said not another word about his own adventures and became utterly self-effacing. He asked about me: my habits and desires, my thoughts, my faith, my past. I shed no light on any of these things, but he persevered. Where had I spent my childhood? How had I learned such excellent French? Did I have family in Holland and, if not, was I lonely? Did I find solace in religion or rely on myself? There was no stopping him. He gave a convincing impression of being fascinated by every facet of my mind, a technique that bespeaks the advanced practitioner. Among the arts of seduction, the gentlest are generally the most effective. But I saw through him all the same.

Were anyone else to take this approach, it would have aroused at least my sympathy, but coming from Seingalt it stirred only annoyance. It was irksome to know that his interest in me was feigned, from which displeasure I realized that I had wanted it to be genuine. And this wish, once discovered, left me in turn disappointed with myself. Is it any wonder that men consider understanding a woman to be invariably a fool's errand? But to sum up: We didn't get on. Undaunted, he persisted in his wide-eyed ways, and presently I decided to take the offensive.

"Are you always so roundabout as to undress a woman intellectually before laying a hand on her body?"

"Her body?" he repeated, as if I had spoken a word of Turkish. "A woman can give her body to anyone. I have no interest in that."

"And you would have me believe you are a man?"

"The challenge I set myself is to win a woman's heart."

"How praiseworthy," I mocked. "And do you win many?"

"Until now? Almost without exception."

He seemed to enjoy my brazenness.

"Wonderful," I continued. "One of these women gives you

her heart. You accept it. I hope you enjoy it. But then? What do you do with the prize? Where do you keep it, once you have it in your possession? You love awhile, and then? Where do you leave it when you go off on your next hunting expedition? Do you nail it to the wall of your trophy room with the rest of the game you've shot, or do you toss it over your shoulder to see where it lands?"

"I have never wronged any of the women I have known. I have never left a single woman to feel ill used."

"Not one?"

"Not one!"

"A pity I am not young or naïve enough to believe you."

"Why should I lie?"

"Goodness," I said, half amused, half exasperated. "Let me think. . . ."

"What has made you so cynical?"

"I have seen enough of what men do with female hearts."

"My lovers and I all parted as friends. You will not find one to say otherwise."

"I am certain you are very courteous in sweeping the pieces together when returning the shattered heart."

"Utterly untrue!"

Like a little boy who has been at the porridge pot he held up his hands, an expression of such innocence that one forgives the child even as he licks the remains from the corners of his mouth.

"When a woman parts from me," he explained, "it must be by mutual agreement. Not in anger. Nor in jealousy."

"And if she doesn't want to? What if she loves you and would keep you?"

"Then it falls to me to find a better man for her, one whose charms outshine my own and compel her to abandon me."

"No broken hearts."

"I'm very clear about that. I see it as a matter of the utmost seriousness. If any beloved of mine were sorrowful at my parting, I would account the whole affair a failure. Not a victory but a defeat."

"Well, thank God you have been spared such a reversal," I said, "unless . . ."— and to heighten the effect I hesitated as long as I dared—"isn't it possible that the women you left simply chose not to tell you of their sorrow?"

"Why should they lie?"

"They loved you, didn't they?"

"Exactly," he said contentedly, as if I had proved his point. "Surely where there is love, one need have no fear of truth?"

"That bit of logic, sir, belies the enormous experience you boast of. Honesty is hardly love's strongest suit."

At this his face dropped.

"Ah," he said, shaking his head, "now you've exposed yourself after all."

"Perhaps a woman would prefer to hold her tongue, taking her fate honorably with a fond farewell. Letting the man believe in his victory, she masks her own defeat."

He considered this, and the thought clearly annoyed him.

"You seem to know much about defeat," he said, with irritation, and then—with some malice—"Have you much experience?"

"Unfortunately."

"I'm sorry, but I shouldn't wonder! You meet good cheer so grimly. What on earth have you against it? It refreshes the spleen and cleanses the blood. Can you hope for happiness when you make love such a grave matter?"

"That's a fine rebuke!" I said. "Just a moment ago it was you, sir, claiming for love the gravity of life and death."

"Fortunately, there are enough women who take their pleasure from it in the same way a man does."

"Have you ever stopped to consider that they might play along to avoid seeming childish? That they would submit to a man rather than be bettered?"

His body stiffened. While he let the scope of the idea sink in, the disbelief in his eyes yielded to determination, and his protest turned angry. Finally he tapped a new vein of strength.

"What kind of woman are you? Would you have me deprived of all pleasure forever? I challenge you: If I have ever wronged one woman, I will make amends for it. I will renounce everything and marry her."

"You think that to marry is to renounce everything. Which of us is the cynic, sir?"

"I would give up my freedom and be hers for the rest of my life."

"You forget, you are a man."

"Love is my religion. The thought that I could hurt someone with it is barbarous."

"So you would do that? End your merry ways, if I could prove that a woman, even one, had fallen victim to her love for you."

"I swear it."

"Take care. I am tempted to keep you to your word."

"One woman, just one from all whom I have loved, who latterly holds me in reproach. I can tell you now: She doesn't exist. You would have better luck turning sulfur into gold."

"The alchemy of love is more dangerous. I have seen it produce stranger transmutations."

"Better still, why not put me to the test yourself, madame? Give me the benefit of your love. Allow me to win you and see whether it pleases—you who have apparently suffered so grievously at the hands of us men."

Words were burning on my lips, but I swallowed them.

"We can make a game of it," he insisted, "and place a wager

on the result, if you like. It might alleviate your boredom for an evening or two."

I assumed an air of indifference, opened a book that was lying on the table, and leafed through it.

"A man who has never wronged a woman," I said, after a while, "how very unusual! How have you managed such a miracle?"

"By placing free will above all else. I want a woman's heart only if she would offer it to me herself. That is not altogether selfless on my part. In my experience, lust is most enjoyable when it is satisfied gladly and avidly. A woman who loves does not hesitate to give herself. She is open in every sense."

"And do you give yourself to her with that same abandon?"

"If only I could," he said, turning suddenly quiet, almost morose. He poked the fire, although it was fairly roaring. "I was deprived of that capacity long ago," he admitted.

"You have been wronged?" I teased. "Even having maintained yourself so selfless!"

"Especially for that reason. Ingratitude is the wages of selflessness."

"Would you have me believe that you are that unique specimen, a man who gives without receiving?"

"I give without expectation."

"Indeed, what could you expect as long as you withheld what is most important?"

"I give enough. I am very generous with my favors."

"I'm glad to hear it. But there are those women who would rather you gave the gift of yourself."

"I know better. I have learned that. I have always been the victim of feminine guile."

"Always?"

"Always."

"From every woman?"

"Without exception."

"You have a strange way of paying compliments, monsieur. No doubt you suspect me as well. So when you invite me to put your love to the test, you are actually asking me to deceive you."

"I find every game more exciting when both players are fully acquainted with the rules."

"Such hardened cynicism! No one ever loved you for yourself?"

He had moved closer and now, while considering his answer, he looked into my eyes as if he could see through my veil. For the first time he frightened me.

"I thought so," he said. I could feel his breath. "Many years ago. . . ."

"And?"

"I was deceived," he said, looking truly abject.

"Very clever, monsieur le Chevalier. But I am smarter. Your whole story is but a transparent ploy to arouse my pity."

"If it were, it would at least have served some purpose." He hung his head and looked up at me through his lashes like a retriever waiting to be rewarded for the game he has fetched.

"Such a charade," I scolded, "such a bare attempt to extort my consolation. Hats off! You almost succeeded. I did feel a momentary impulse to prove myself a trustworthy woman. How many times has that gambit borne fruit?"

"I've lost count," he said, with a merry affect, to suggest the performance was over.

I laughed. "We are worthy opponents."

"That surely proves you must have once been disappointed in the same way?"

I remained silent.

"And your own story must have won many a man's heart."

"Your life is a comedy, monsieur. Your little sorrows are merely entr'actes. My drama is a touch more serious. A man can turn his setbacks to advantage. Life always gives him another chance. For a woman, every blow is devastating."

"Go on then, speak. Let your story be a lesson to me."

"It has never been offered to a living soul and never shall be."

"Tell it then for the first time to someone who loves you."

"I will, to be sure. On the day when someone's love shows itself to be without condition, I will reveal it."

"I shall make it then my business to prove myself on that day."

"It is bound to be a disagreeable one for you, monsieur."

At that moment a cry went up outside our window. Immediately afterward, something thudded onto the ground and we heard the splintering of wood. Seingalt ran out, and I after him. A gust of wind had swept up one of the carriages and smashed it against the wall of the bakehouse. The coachman, who had been inside it, sheltering from the rain, now lay on the ground under one of the shafts. He screamed for help. We were the first to reach him. He was badly injured. The broken frame of the carriage impaled his leg. Blood pumped profusely from the long wound and the large artery that had been laid bare. I lifted my skirts and tore off three thick strips. I ordered the chevalier to press the flesh together as hard as he could. He hesitated. My sangfroid seemed to astonish him. I bandaged the wound so tightly that the bleeding stopped and then removed as many of the splinters as possible. Finally the unfortunate man was carried off and someone went to fetch a surgeon.

Once the driver seemed to have been saved, I became aware—as one does, belatedly—of the fright I had suffered. I trembled. For a moment Seingalt and I stood there alone in the night. He embraced me cautiously. I allowed it. The horses,

which were hitched to a rail, reared as if sensing some impend-
ing disaster, and a second later a new squall was tugging at the
branches and roofs. My dress swelled like a sail. I lost my footing
and was dragged several yards. Seingalt tried to restrain me but
was caught in the same current. Ending up sprawled in the mud
together, we could neither of us keep from laughing. Seingalt's
blond wig slipped down almost over his eyes. He took it off.

Beneath it, he had short black curls.

His eyes glinted in the light of a hanging lantern, between
them the sharp silhouette of his nose. A gust of wind took my
breath away.

"You don't believe that a man can really care for you," he
said, leaning up against me and brushing my shoulder tenderly
with his cheek. The practiced seducer was not slow to regain his
footing. "Obviously you have never known one who was worthy of your love."

"Obviously."

"It is incumbent on me to be the first."

"The game is not worth the candle, monsieur."

I stood up and went inside without his assistance. I excused
myself, saying that I needed to make myself presentable.
Unseen, I collected my cloak and descended to the kitchen,
where the coachmen had gathered. None would take me back
to Amsterdam. My departure could not, however, be postponed
any longer. I walked to the stables and chose a strong stallion.
The groom refused to saddle it, unwilling to risk one of his animals on a night like this. For my part, I have braved far worse
than his animals had. I mounted the horse bareback and spurred
it on with nothing but my shoes. I rode it the way I learned to
ride at Pasiano, holding tight to the mane.

It was ungodly along the Amstel. The waves broke over the
river road. Seven souls perished that night. But the moon was

full. The clouds raced across the sky. I pressed on as if in a trance. Along the way, I lost my veil to the wind. The rain beat against my face and ran down my cheeks, but I did not slow my pace. There was no one to see me. For that night the cold was mask enough, and I delighted in it.

4

THERE WAS ANOTHER year when everything changed.

In the spring of '42, the Countess of Montereale returned to Pasiano earlier than usual. We were asked to prepare the house in the very first week of April, and when she arrived from Venice she brought a sizable retinue of artists and workmen. The permanent staff of Pasiano was summoned and told that we would spend the whole summer working under the direction of the Venetians. They wasted no time in starting to order us about. We had to take down the curtains and the paintings, lower the chandeliers, and roll up the carpets. The woodwork would be repainted and the walls lined with embroidered silk; the ponds, so much more agreeable drained, had their basins scraped clean and painted pale blue and were filled with clear water. Two new fountains were installed, and small shrubs were planted on the lawn in the precise lines dictated by the French style. Once the citrus trees had been transplanted into new tubs, work was begun to transform the orangery into a reception hall.

The countess herself was very busy. She rarely left her rooms, and I was unsuccessful in my first attempts to see her. Two secretaries I had never seen before baldly refused to admit me. One morning in some desperation I took the breakfast tray from her lady's maid, entered her bedchamber without knocking, jumped onto her bed, and woke her with effusive kisses. It took her a moment to recover, but when she did, she was delighted to see me and began to tell me her news.

Adriana de Montereale had made an excellent match. All the care, time, and money that had been invested in improving her position in Venice would bear fruit this autumn. The wedding, which would admit her to the city's nobility, was to be held in September, and the countess planned a reception at Pasiano that would be as magnificent as any party held on the Canal Grande.

As the countess explained all this, her anxiety was more apparent than her pleasure. The affair sounded more a trial than a festivity, and the mere thought of the work to be done in the coming months brought her to tears. I pushed her back down onto her pillows, rubbed her temples, and in the candor of our old intimacy said that a lady of her wisdom and tranquillity surely had no reason to be deranged merely to satisfy the whims of the city.

"Ah, child." She sighed, enjoying the massage. I felt her skin relax beneath my fingers. "You are good and simple. Thank God you live here and not in Venice. You can't imagine how malicious people can be."

"In Venice?" I couldn't believe my ears. "Where everyone is so happy?"

"Of the sway of envy there, you have no idea, and it only worsens the higher one's station. Men acquire their jobs and status at the assemblies, but that's just half the battle. Power depends on reputation, the opinion of those who matter in so-called cultured circles. This is where the women enter the fray.

"The ballrooms of Venice are battlefields; every drawing room that seems a tranquil bay is in fact a harbor for frigates lying in wait. One dances, drinks, and makes merry courtship, but meanwhile a battle is raging. The victor rules the seas for the whole season ahead. In that period, the rest can only seek relative advantage, making such propitious alliances as they can. That's when the warfare turns merciless. All means are justified. For women, the terms of engagement are ruthlessly simple: Everything comes down to appearance. Beauty is the only armament with which the ladies contest one another."

She continued to paint her martial tableau as I continued to massage her. It seemed exaggerated to me, but the problem was far from my concerns. I was free. So far as I knew, no one had ever judged me, and such woes seemed quite foreign. I was fourteen besides, an age when a well-built young man was much more appealing than the most wellborn beanpole. To be governed in one's taste by appearances seemed perfectly natural and healthy.

My reaction must have struck her as dangerously frivolous, because the countess sat up and seized my hands, as if caught by a sudden spasm.

"You have no idea how cruel it can be," she said, resting my hands on her shoulders. For a moment it felt as if I were the protective elder and she the vulnerable girl. "Yes, everything glitters at those parties, gleaming and sparkling like the treasures under the domes of San Marco. But just as you can't tell from the gold, enamel, and porphyry decorating those sacred walls how much blood was spilt in the cities of the Levant to acquire them, it's just as easy to forget that every soft laugh pealing through the halls of the palazzi has been won at a terrible cost. How could you know, dear child, that to receive an invitation to a particular soirée can mean salvation. . . . What am I saying? To be excluded can destroy a *life*! Only last season there was the awful sight of a son of the—no, I swore that name would never cross my lips again, but you may be certain it was one of the leading families. Anyway, the poor boy had found the love of his life. She could have been a picture of a girl, really—no one denied that—but for a birthmark, a horrid purplish-red thing that extended so far up her throat that even the highest collars couldn't hide it. As soon as their engagement became known, tongues started wagging. The post that had been promised the young man—as ambassador to Cyprus—went to someone else, merely because his fiancée was considered unsuitable to represent the Serenissima and its citizens. Because of that birthmark and for no other reason, the boy's father denied the young couple his blessing. That same night they sailed out into the lagoon together and drowned themselves in the swamp beyond Mazzorbo."

She fell silent. I screwed my eyes shut and shuddered, as if the poor unfortunates might float up to the surface in the corner of the room.

"Why on earth would anyone take his life over such a thing as love?"

"Dear child, what other reason could incite such an awful deed?" she said, with sincere incomprehension. Then, as if having only just remembered our differences of age and station, she kissed me on the forehead, calming me like a lapdog.

"I have prayed, prayed every day, and I am still praying that Adriana might survive to her wedding. I've had masses said. And now it seems—yes, now it really does seem as though by God's grace—"

"But why tempt fate?" I asked. "Adriana could have grown up here, at Pasiano, where we have nothing to fear. If Venice is such a nest of vipers, why do you return every winter?"

Quietly she said, "Why? Why indeed. One can become a country recluse, but in fact that takes even more courage."

I laughed because I couldn't imagine anywhere less demanding of courage than Pasiano, but the countess insisted.

"Turning down a path that no one else follows, that requires more strength than I have been able to muster in this life."

I dressed her; then off I went to help around the house. But from that day the simple pleasure I used to take in my chores eluded me as the preparations continued.

AT THE START of August, purveyors of wine brought cases from Champagne and the island of Madeira. Every evening new musicians came to the house, playing their repertoire by way of audition as we lay in the fields to recover from the day's hard work. Two weeks later saw the arrival of a battalion of cooks, cases full of silverware, and the Chinese porcelain the family used in Venice. Seamstresses came to measure the house servants for new livery.

Toward the end of the month, Adriana arrived with her teacher, Monsieur de Pompignac. While she strode from the carriage to the steps, the Frenchman scuttled around her nervously, as though trying to add the last dabs of civilization before delivering his creation to her ancestral home.

Old Count Antonio came from Milan soon after. I had seen him several times before, but on those occasions he had never noticed me. Instead of moving in with the countess, he took up residence in the opposite wing. One afternoon he summoned me there and took me on his lap. His smiles and playfulness were not so comforting as his wife's, and I broke away as soon as I could. That same day, five new coaches were delivered, each with a fresh team, to transport the guests. The courier L'Aigle, a handsome young man, arrived with fourteen large hams from Parma. Someone came from L'Aquila with saffron, and a Slovenian brought chalk for the rhubarb. Every morning you heard the death cries of animals being slaughtered at the surrounding farms. Around midday the carcasses arrived in the kitchen. My mother made sure that the best cuts were properly salted and preserved, and the scraps minced for pastries. My father led an expedition to the mountaintop near Zoldo, between Cadore and Ampezzo. At this time of year he and his men had to climb to great heights, but in the end they brought back enough ice so that even after the cellars had been filled there was behind the stables still a pile of snow that refused to melt. On hot days the grooms went there to cool off. They made a slope just for me and found no end of pleasure in watching me climb the mound in my chemise and skirt and slide down on a wooden plank.

I came to enjoy all the estate's new business. I couldn't remember so many delightful diversions since the year the fair had come to Conegliano. Those carefree months at my beloved Pasiano have never left me and, please God, they never shall.

THE PEAK of my contentment was yet to come. It arrived in the first week of September on a farmer's cart that was almost lost among the ornate carriages that had been coming and going all day long. I was watching all this grandeur from a hiding place between the kitchen and the outbuildings when two youths caught my eye by jumping off the back of a cart outside the gate. They slipped a few soldi to the farmer who had brought them, brushed the oats off their clothes, and strode into the forecourt no less assuredly than if they had just stepped out of a gilded carriage. My laughter must have betrayed my position, because one pointed me out and nudged the other, who doffed his hat. For me! He raised it, holding it up for a moment, and nodded slightly, fixing me with his eyes the whole time. I have enjoyed many courtesies since then, but on my deathbed only this first one will appear before me. It made me wonder whether anyone had ever actually noticed me before. In that same instant, the youth burst out laughing as well. He put a finger to his lips as if to beseech my discretion about the humbleness of their conveyance, and with a wink he sealed our pact as conspirators.

Bold as brass, the two of them stepped up to my father and gave him their names. They were obviously on the guest list, because he welcomed them, just as he had done with the others who belonged. A servant led them into the salon, where there were cakes and cold drinks to enjoy until their rooms had been prepared. As soon as my new friends had climbed the stairs, I ran over to my father and tried to gather from his list who they were. He guessed my intentions.

"Seminarians," he teased, but in the end he gave me their names: Francesco and Giacomo Casanova. My father intoned the latter's name with a mocking tip of his own hat, having obviously noticed the boy's courtesy. Inflamed by the taunt, I turned on my heel and went off to look for my mother. I found her in the basement, assigning the rooms. She was standing in the main corridor before the large board where the keys to the different rooms hung on hooks. She had her own list and crossed off the names as they arrived. She jotted each down on a slip of paper and hung it up on the hook by the number of the room the countess had reserved for that guest. Her estimation of my new friends was clearly less lofty than their own, because she had tucked them away in the farthest recesses of the house, three floors up. My heart sank. I never went up there in ordinary times, but especially now, servants' children having been strictly banned from the house for the duration of the festivities, the attic was completely inaccessible.

At that moment my mother was informed that the canon of Treviso had arrived. She crossed his name off on her list and transcribed it on a piece of paper. A suite of rooms on the first floor had been reserved for him alone, but my mother thought that was a waste for a single man. She paused to think whether there wasn't a more modest alternative still befitting his station. I suggested a room in the east wing facing the garden. Its doors opened onto a terrace not thirty yards from our own cottage . . .

A footman came up to announce the arrival of the next guest, and by now my mother's head was spinning.

I offered to hang the note with the canon's name next to the right key.

MY NEW FRIEND was no doubt overjoyed when they showed him his room early that evening. He might have been disappointed to be parted from his brother (now forced to share the attic with the canon), but Giacomo would have adjusted to the change soon enough once he realized that he was sharing a hall with Venetian aristocrats. At any rate, he threw open the terrace doors with a joyful flourish and took in his surroundings with satisfaction. I thought he might have been looking for me, but before I could emerge from the shrubbery where I had been observing him, he had already turned his back. He broke into a run with an equestrian call and leaped onto the bed as onto a mount, seemingly to have reclined there until dinnertime. Unwilling to risk disturbing him, I contented myself with the thought that he would soon find the bunch of lavender I had laid under his pillow.

EARLY THE NEXT MORNING, finding the doors of his room ajar, I stepped in through the rippling curtains. Giacomo awoke when I put the tray down on his bed stand. I poured his chocolate and drew his attention to the dish with fruit confit. I had picked the red currants myself, at my aunt's in Belluno, but thought better of saying so and seeming presumptuous. He soaked his brioche in the chocolate and took a bite, without a word.

I just stood there, waiting, hoping his eyes had perhaps not yet adjusted to the light.

I had expected him to recognize me from the previous afternoon, but he ate impassively as he looked at me. Whenever the sheet slid down from his chest, he pulled it up to his chin again, as if my standing there embarrassed him.

"Is your bed satisfactory?" I asked at last.

"Entirely," he said. "Did you make it up?"

I nodded. And then there was silence again.

Suddenly I became aware of how I must have looked in his eyes. I was barefoot, as always, in a skirt and a chemise, which I seemed not to have buttoned properly.

"What is your name?" he asked.

"Lucia!" I couldn't help but sound a little huffy. "I am the housekeeper's daughter!" And to make up for my tone, I chirpily offered more than I had been asked. "I don't have any brothers or sisters and I'm fourteen."

"Fourteen," he said. "A fine age." He blushed.

"Since you don't have a manservant, I'll serve you myself. I hope it will be satisfactory."

"I'm certain of it."

His reticence annoyed me. How could someone so bold one day seem so shy the next? I was torn between two unpleasant prospects: continue to face his awkward gaze or leave and put him out of mind. Instead, by some impulse that popped into my head, I sat down on the end of his bed. Startled at first, he jerked his legs up and the sheet fell down, leaving him almost naked. The panic with which he recovered it and drew up his knees set me giggling.

At the same time I had some intimation that this was a moment of great importance in my life. I had no words for it, but somehow I knew I would remember it. It was a new feeling yet instantly familiar, as if something I had known since birth had suddenly occurred to me. What I realized in that instant was that *I* had robbed Giacomo, the same swaggering boy of the day before, of his courage. Intuitively it followed that we could never be friends in the way I had always had friends up till then. There was something between us that would keep us at a wary distance just as surely as it drew us together. And although, or perhaps because, it was the first time I had ever felt that way, I also believed that it was irrevocable. That I would never again be able simply to play with all and sundry. This awareness pained and pleased me in equal measure.

Finally he started giggling too. The ice was broken. I passed him his dressing gown and sat awhile on his bed. When my parents came in, they apologized for my behavior. To my humiliation, they told Giacomo that I was as virtuous and pure as an angel. My candor and informality were entirely due to my innocence; I was still a child, wholly unacquainted with certain aspects of adulthood. They spoke out of pure decency, but they might just as well have told him that I washed every morning in pig's swill. My parents chastized me as a child, lovingly, without explaining the nature of my offense. I left to get dressed. By some great good fortune Giacomo didn't hold it against me, as I would discover later when I overheard him speaking with Francesco in the rose garden.

"She's beautiful. She's obedient. She's pious. She's the picture of health, white skin and black eyes."

"Sounds perfect!"

"You'd think so," Giacomo said, suddenly gloomy. "She *would* be perfect, except for one thing."

"And that is?"

"She's too young."

He was in earnest, but his brother could only laugh. "A marvelous imperfection!"

5

THE MAD RIDE along the Amstel in the bracing rain had focused my mind. Long-forgotten scars contracted in the cold. The danger kept me alert as well as exhilarated. I saw the path I needed to take and all its pitfalls. Gleaming in the distance were the beacons of Amsterdam. For years I had thought of this city as my final destination. That night, though, I realized my journey was not yet over.

WITH EACH BREATH we take, all our dreams—every birth and every death—slip farther beyond our powers of comprehension. Of all our failings, this is the most troubling. Our lives are subject to cosmic and microcosmic processes beyond our reckoning. This is a terrifying fact; to know it is one thing but to long beyond reason for some way of influencing these processes— that is something else.

The desire is for magic.

This is what the alchemists are searching for. They strive to transform things. They write the Delphic dictum *Know thyself!* on their mirrors and set to work, trying with burners and retorts to use one substance to turn a second one into yet a third. I know nothing of alchemy, but I've learned this much: The tangible can be reshaped only by the intangible.

The only thing that can change reality is the mind. I have discovered this in the laboratory of my own life. If one would change things, one needn't touch them; one need only see them differently. Let a thing catch a particular light for a moment, that's all, like the engraving on the back of the glass. Suddenly it is transformed for all time. Once you've seen it you can hardly believe you never noticed it before.

This is the elusive cosmic process.

I have known it.

If love is magic, then I am a magician.

ONCE THE STORM had died down, I set to work. It was a question of changing or being changed. I sent the chevalier an apology for my abrupt departure and suggested that we meet again. An answer did not come at once, as his affairs had taken him to The Hague, but on the last day of the month I received news that Jacques de Seingalt had taken up residence nearby in the Doelenstraat. I informed him that I would receive him at my home. I did add, for the sake of clarity, that—Holland being a more liberal place than the rest of Europe—Dutch girls are brought up ever mindful of the dangers that might beset a woman out about town. As a consequence of this universal awareness, the custom is to receive a gentleman at home, and no one sees cause for a scandal in women entertaining guests without chaperones.

HE PRESENTED HIMSELF that very evening. Although he had obviously not been expecting such a modest flat, he treated me with all the customary courtesies. Not a word betrayed his surprise at my humble circumstances, though his conversation was somewhat milder than it had been on our previous encounter. I was prepared to attribute that to a growing ease and familiarity. Despite myself, I too felt more at ease. I had asked the cook of the Cow's Head to prepare a small supper. When it was brought to the house, Seingalt insisted on settling the account with the boy. He did this quickly and naturally, so that I felt not the slightest awkwardness.

His approach was more cautious this time. His tone was just as playful and amorous, but he no longer probed so insistently. The meagerness of my possessions forming such a sharp contrast to my bearing, he seemed not so curious to inquire about my adventures. I took the opportunity to question him about his.

"Do you suppose the years have changed you?" I asked, beginning the match.

"Not years but people."

"How did they manage that?"

"By revealing to me their want of depth."

"So you would account yourself more profound—cleverer at least?"

I poured some wine. It smelled tart, but that didn't seem to bother him.

"One needn't be so artful to get the better of most people," he continued. "They are only too eager to be deceived. You get farther by being brazen, actually. No, I have changed on account of having lost respect."

"For them?"

"Yes, in part, but consequently for myself as well. I don't deny that I have taken advantage of their willingness to be deluded. Mind you, I have felt no compunction whenever it seemed necessary to cheat dunces, rogues, or fools."

Clearly he took pleasure in recalling his villainies. As he

recounted several elaborate deceptions he had perpetrated across Europe, the grin never faded from his face.

It is true: People seem at pains to be swindled. I have turned that fact to my own advantage often enough. Oddly, it is the advance of science in this century that has torn many souls apart from within. Here the simpleminded—and I was certainly once one of them—trusting only to what they feel, are at some advantage. Their concern is as ever for the things that affect their daily life; as for mysteries, only those they encounter within it matter. They respond to these things impulsively, as they have for generations, and whatever they can't reckon in this way they leave in the hands of Providence. The new discoveries, however, contradict these emotions; even the existence of God no longer seems a certainty. Those who immerse themselves in these revelations have grown confused. They have their doubts but do not yet dare put all their trust in reason, unable to abandon their faith entirely, even as it abandons them. Such folk remind me of a huntsman I once saw on the river. He had ventured out onto the ice too late in the season and was floating downstream, his left foot planted on one floe, his right foot on another. Unable to decide where to stand, he drowned. Many thoughtful people are likewise adrift, trying to keep a footing in both reason and emotion. They try to use science to find proof of a spiritual reality. This is the key to the success that charlatans enjoy, not among the backward but with the educated classes. And so, claim as they might to be enlightened by reason, the well-schooled are but a step away from drowning in confusion.

Seingalt rehearsed his description of various simpletons whose folly had profited him. He seemed practiced, even expectant, about the charms of these burlesque anecdotes, but—confining my interest to the man himself, not his knavish tricks—I cut him short.

"Don't you agree," I ventured, "that, when traveling, it is se-
ductively simple to adopt a new guise?" He looked at me for a
moment but did not dare ask what I meant or how I had come
to this knowledge. For a moment I was afraid that my forth-
rightness had aroused his suspicions. But then I continued.
"For me, at least, it has always been a tremendous comfort to
know that one can always leave everything behind and—if
necessary—slough off one's whole existence, as a snake sheds
its skin between two stones."

"It's true, a new arrival can always pretend to be someone
else. It is precisely when no one knows you that everyone is so
keen to fit you into some category. That's a human need, so
most are only too glad of the convenience of your telling them
what to make of you. As for the occasional skeptic who may
require proof, a simple letter of introduction with a grand name
on it will suffice. Theoretically, it's quite possible to be a physi-
cian in one country, an opera singer in the next, and a lawyer
three days down the road."

"And you would have us in Holland believe that France has
sent you to the Amsterdam bourse as a banker?" I teased. "You
must hold our intelligence especially low, not to have devised
some more plausible identity for your arrival."

"Fortunately, my story has the advantage of truth about it,
and I have as evidence bills of exchange from the bank worth
twenty million francs—"

"Please don't bother, monsieur. I don't have a sou to pledge,
so financial matters are of no interest to me. You have my blessing. But I do not like to be deceived. I tell you that now. Your
name, for instance, is French, but your accent betrays quite a different origin."

He admitted as much, and I listened impassively when he
told me his real name. He explained that he had only recently

exchanged his Italian surname for a French one better suited to his service to the state.

"Being of no consequence or influence in your affairs is then a blessing, I suppose, for otherwise I could never escape the thought that your attentions were conferred with a purpose," I said.

"As if winning your heart were not a purpose of the greatest importance!"

"Rest assured that only Truth can win it. All others die before the gates."

He burst out laughing.

"Ah, there *is* another truth. I suspected as much," I said.

"Perhaps you prefer this one."

Whereupon he dished up a ludicrous tale of an elderly Parisienne, a certain Madame d'Urfé, who having succumbed to occult delusions believed herself in possession of the philosopher's stone. So enchanted was she by Seingalt's arts that she took refuge in the hope that after her death he would resurrect her soul in a male body. To secure the funds necessary for this miracle, she had sent him to Amsterdam with instructions to sell her substantial shares in the Dutch East India Company.

He stared at me shamelessly.

"Every last word of that is true," he said, "but does it sound any more plausible? Do you see now why I think it folly, this enthrallment to the truth, when a dash of fantasy is so much more agreeably credible?"

"Touché," I admitted wholeheartedly. "You're right; facts are generally more peculiar than invention." Life had taught me that, long before Seingalt's appearance at my flat. "In any case," I resumed, "it's one more name I can add to the long list of women you have deceived. Poor Madame d'Urfé."

"As far as women are concerned, the deception is mutual and therefore beyond reproach; where love is involved, both parties are duped. As for Madame d'Urfé: The ethics are quite different when one is dealing with fools. They know no shame, and their vanity is beyond description. To cheat a fool is to avenge reason: quite honorable."

"She doesn't believe that you love her?"

"Why, no, she believes me a sorcerer."

"And are you?"

"Certainly, for those who wish it before all else. Mind you, I do not toy with their confidence. I should be very much chagrined if you formed that impression, madame," he said, in all seriousness. "Nor is their belief that I can help them altogether ill-founded. Over the years I have become proficient in many useful arts, such as chemistry, which enables me to carry out impressive demonstrations, and cryptography, which allows me to unravel the most intricate of codes. Also, for my own private cultivation, I have studied the cabala, as well as the works of Ramon Llull and Hermes Trismegistus."

"All these arts to heighten your trickery—a most studied charlatan."

"What knowledge I have amassed has been purely for my own benefit—you will have to take my word for that. I have an insatiable curiosity. If it might also be turned to the advantage of others, all the better."

"Most noble," I sneered.

"I have always accounted nobility a puffed-up virtue, never so well esteemed as it is when acquired natively. I have never professed to be part of humanity's just minority. I lead no one to believe in my powers; rather, it is this day and age that afflicts so many with the need for something to believe. I don't take that lightly. Indeed, I owe my own life to having once been needfully deceived myself. I was eight years old. . . ." His voice softened as he searched for words. "Eight years old. I remember looking down and seeing blood dripping on the tiles. I was counting the drops, following with my eyes each one that fell, transfixed, until suddenly I realized that the blood was mine. It was coming from my nose. I stood in the corner by the window and called faintly for my grandmother. She washed my face with cold water. Seeing how profusely I was bleeding, she took me to the shack of an old woman outside the city. She was sitting on a bed with a black cat in her arms: a witch, I was given to understand. My grandmother gave her some money. The witch put me in a chest. By then I had lost so much blood my head was spinning. Too far gone to be scared, I just lay there with a rag pressed against my nose, listening to the goings-on around me: singing, shouting, mad laughter and crying, and regular blows against the sides of the chest. Finally the witch pulled me out. The bleeding had stopped. She hugged me, undressed me, and laid me on the bed. Then she burned some herbs and, catching the smoke in a sheet, she wrapped me up in it. She gave me five delicious sweets. The bleeding would not resume, she said, as long as I never spoke to anyone of that night, but if I betrayed a single word of what had happened, my veins would empty themselves and I would die. She let me go with the promise that I would be visited that same night by an enchanting, beautiful lady on whom my happiness would depend. And so I was. She appeared toward morning. I saw—or thought I did, not that it matters—a dazzling beauty emerge from the fireplace. She was wearing a glittering jeweled crown and a magnificent dress with a wide hoop. She delivered herself of a long speech of which I understood not a word and, with a kiss on my head, left the way she had come."

He looked at me expectantly, as if surprised that I had not interrupted the story.

"Then I fell asleep." He had lowered his voice, almost to a whisper. He took my hand. Through my veil he could not possibly have seen the effect of his story, but having made a fair guess he wanted to reassure me.

Never had I known a man capable of such empathy.

"The cures for serious ills are not always to be found at the apothecary's," he said. "Having since come to understand that, I never trifle with the faith others invest in me. Once someone has given you her trust, the merest suggestion can be enough to devastate or heal."

I was no longer able to control myself and began to sob with great heaves of my chest. He was shocked and could not have suspected why this, of all his tall stories, should have touched me so profoundly. He sat there like a little boy startled at the consequences of his mischief, uncertain what to do.

"Many things that exist only in the imagination," he said, "later become real."

I tried with all my might to catch my breath and calm myself to prevent his going on, but I was struck dumb. My mind raced ahead to the potential consequences of every word I might utter, and the fear of these seized my throat. Every unspoken word seemed dangerous. It was all I could do to clench my teeth and sit still, not even bothering to wipe my cheeks, hoping he might think my sorrowful outburst but a passing fit of emotion more common to women than men.

"Evidence of that was provided again eight years later, when I recognized in the face of my very first love the beauty who had visited me as a child."

"A pretty picture," I said, finally regaining my composure, fortified by annoyance at his prattle. "But falling in love with a face one imagines to remember from a dream? That hardly seems the stuff of profound affection."

This clearly unnerved him. Doubtless this tender song had melted many a woman's heart. Now it was perfectly clear that not a single word he uttered had gone unweighed in his balance of conquest.

"If your love goes no deeper than a face resembling a dream, my pity to the poor girl so endowed. Had she no qualities of her own?"

"You misconceive me. . . ."

"Why did you love her then?"

"How am I to remember that? I am speaking of my first love, and many have come and gone since."

"Yes, of course," I said. "Perhaps I should ask what *she* saw in *you*. That's something the male memory generally manages to retain, I find."

We spoke of other things for a while, but the friendly atmosphere was dissipated. I announced wordlessly that his visit was drawing to a close with his goal still unachieved. It was late, and I was expecting Giovanna and Danaë at any moment, to hand over my share of their earnings. By the end of the night the Parmesan pair could look very tired, spent, and trashy. Not wanting to subject the chevalier to their slatternliness, I said goodbye and showed him to the door. He was already in the street when something occurred to him, and he turned back to face me.

"I loved my first love because she poured me a glass of water."

"Water the basis for love?" I teased. "I should hardly wonder it didn't last."

"One day she poured me some water. An ordinary glass, but she held it up to the light as if it were a crystal chalice. I looked, but no matter how I tried, I couldn't see what she saw in it. 'Water takes on the shape of the vessel.' Her voice was full of awe. 'Just now it was the shape of the jug; now it's the shape of the glass.' She said it as if drawing my attention to a wonder. I laughed at her. She looked up shocked. Tears filled her eyes. 'It seemed such a miracle. It has always surprised me. The water in the stream is shaped like the banks. In my hands it takes on the shape of my palms.' She was quite distraught to imagine that I thought her foolish. 'I take no offense,' she sobbed. 'It's just . . . I always thought it so beautiful, and from now on it will just be ordinary.'"

Monsieur le Chevalier de Seingalt was still standing in the street with his hat in hand. It was raining, but he didn't seem to have noticed. His eyes were still trying to find mine through my veil.

"Why should a miracle be any less of one just because someone else can't see it?"

6

MY PARENTS got on well with Giacomo. They were still talking to him when I reentered his room. I had washed in the meantime and put up my hair. I was wearing a clean dress and had put on shoes, not something I was used to.

"Is that better?"

I turned around and reaped their applause. Giacomo patted his coverlet, a sign that I was now welcome to sit on his bed.

"Dressed and all?" I said haughtily. "No, sir, it's all well and good as long as you don't think about it, but sitting down on a bed in my best clothes—no, that's too grand for me."

My answer seemed to please everyone.

"She's a lot nicer like this than in her blouse, isn't she?" asked my mother. The young abbé looked me over from head to toe, and I could tell he didn't agree. When a footman arrived to tend his hair, we left him alone, but later that day, when I made his bed, I left a vase with fresh flowers on the table with a small brass bell.

THE NEXT MORNING he rang for his breakfast. When I delivered it, I came as he liked to see me. I was much surer of myself than I had been the day before and climbed unbidden onto the foot of his bed. We talked that way for quite a while. He too seemed more at ease, and when I rolled over onto my stomach, propping myself up on my elbows, he came and lay down beside me. He told me he had recently completed his study of law in Padua, just before his seventeenth birthday. The patriarch of Venice himself had already tonsured the prodigy and conferred the minor orders on him.

I asked whether he was planning to enter a monastery, which question he answered by blowing into my chemise so that it billowed out and gave him a better view. I lashed out at him and we wrestled until we were both out of breath. That was all. Then we lay side by side for a while until we recovered.

I told him about my grandfather and the mirrors in the grand salon. Suddenly I felt his hand on my breast. I was startled and moved back, but the hand followed. I was not yet fully developed. I was aware of that, but never so painfully. I had no doubt that I had disappointed him, and I blushed. I could already hear his conversation with his brother Francesco. In a matter of seconds, I imagined every word of their exchange, their howls of derision among the rosebushes. My cheerfulness dissolved. I grew so obviously confused that Giacomo finally released me. I immediately regretted my actions. My earlier embarrassment was as nothing to what I felt now. To make amends, I moved closer. I took his hand and told him that I hadn't meant to be unfriendly. He reassured me.

"You are innocent," he said, as if that were news. "It's just that you're free and not prim at all. Such an easy way can be terribly confusing to a young man."

He ate the rolls I sugared for him while telling him about the animals in the fields and the overseer's dogs and my adventures in the forests around Pasiano. He interrupted me in mid-sentence, as if he hadn't been listening, to ask whether I was cold and wouldn't I be more comfortable if I crawled in under the covers beside him.

"Wouldn't that be difficult for you?"

"Not at all. I worry only that your mother might come in."

"She wouldn't think badly of it."

"No?"

"I'm not stupid. And you're sensible. And a priest."

I snuggled up next to him and continued my story, but it was as if he were deaf. He couldn't concentrate on a word I said, and I soon tired of talking without a listener. It was already ten o'clock and I told him that I wanted to get up to be sure of avoiding Count Antonio, who sometimes crossed the terrace at that hour.

"I'm leaving now," I said, when Giacomo insisted that I stay to help him dress, "because I have no curiosity at all about seeing you upright."

He groaned.

Apparently he was to have a conversation with my parents later that day, though they revealed this to me only much later. He professed his conviction that I was an angel incarnate and certain to fall victim to the first rogue to present himself. He promised them it would not be he, on account of his having resolved to befriend me chastely, a promise he would make good, though they could hardly have expected it. My parents, anxious simple folk, were taken at once by his chivalrous words and agreed they could think of no one to whom they would sooner entrust my virtue. With what degree of calculation I cannot tell, they accepted the young priest's offer to become my teacher and protector. They were hopeful that, while maintaining my innocence, he might instruct me in the dangers of youth.

.   .   .

WHEN MY MOTHER walked into his room from the garden the next day, she seemed perfectly content to find me on the bed. She even kissed me, calling me the consolation of their old age, and thanked Giacomo for his moral tutelage. The young priest said that I could not yet appreciate how lucky I was to have parents who were so kind and trusting.

About this, at least, he would be proved right.

With their encouragement, I no longer felt awkward in Giacomo's presence. During the week of the festivities, I was in his room every morning; he spent the rest of the day at the parties and excursions the countess had arranged. Sometimes in the evening I would see him briefly on the terrace, but generally I had to wait until the next morning, when I threw myself onto his bed and covered his face with kisses.

The week of festivities ended with a large display of fireworks, lit from diverse places in the hills around Pasiano. My father was in charge of the big sparklers and cascades that were to be lit close to the wooded bank north of the house. I was there with him and marveled at the spectacle that was about to begin.

"Here she goes!" my father cheered, holding the tinder under the first fuse. "Just say, 'Goodbye, dear guests, thanks for nothing and see you never!'"

It was as if that first salvo woke me up. The awareness that in the morning my playmate would be leaving with the other guests suddenly erupted. I leaped up, shrieking. My father, shocked by the violence of my reaction, tried with all his might to restrain me, but as he was obliged to fix his attention on the pyrotechnics, I managed to break free. In a panic, I ran across fields ablaze in red, yellow, and blue all around me. Burning debris fell from the sky to my left and right, but I was heedless. I raced toward the mansion, lit up in the distance. The guests had gathered at the top of the steps, some yelling warnings to take cover, but I ran on through the shower of smoldering stars. At the house I fell to my knees at the feet of the countess. Before I could speak, she had surmised the cause of my distress because Giacomo had pushed his way through the crowd and was bending over me solicitously.

"Am I really to be so blessed, my dear"—she laughed—"as to see history repeat itself?" She exchanged knowing looks with my mother, who had rushed up now as well, whereupon I heard Count Antonio make a coarse remark. For a moment I was vexed to feel that everyone had realized what was happening to me before I did. But the discomfort passed when the countess asked Giacomo whether he would be so gracious as to stay behind and keep us company at Pasiano for the whole of September.

TIME WAS NOW OURS, and I took him to all the corners of my world. We left before dawn to see the deer in Codopé and walked on to Azanello. There we made a fire in the ruins to toast the bread my mother had given us. The rest of the day we wandered through the fields or tried to lure the horses in the meadow near Cornizzai, so that we could climb onto their backs, holding tight to their manes until they bucked and we fell off, screaming with laughter.

These days passed like a dream in which everything strange seems familiar. I thought I had discovered all there was to know about Pasiano in my fourteen years, but as I showed it to Giacomo it was as if I were aware of my home for the first time. Some of the places I had always loved disappointed me now, seeing them as they must have appeared to him. Try as I might to explain what I had found so beautiful, I was myself unpersuaded even as I spoke, and I heard the conviction draining from my words. Other things never really noticed before suddenly glowed when they caught his eye. One moment I felt sorrow, as if I had betrayed my old self; the next I was overjoyed to find my perspective enlarged. My world magnified because my consciousness was doubled. Of this I was quite certain. No longer limited to my own thoughts, my awareness suddenly included everything he believed and felt, desired and hoped.

In the heat of the afternoon, we swam in the lake on the Rivarotta to cool ourselves, then lay on the shore to dry. In those precious moments I asked him questions. I wanted to know everything. Sometimes, when he had told me a story, I asked him to tell it to me again, from start to finish, scared that I might have missed some detail or would forget it by nightfall. The next afternoon, still not trusting to my recollection, I asked to hear it all yet again.

The compass of his experience seemed extraordinary, and to hear of his adventures made my head swim. I had never imagined such a varied life except once at the spring fair in Sacile, when a street singer recounted the adventures of Gil Blas, which his assistants enacted as tableaux. At Pasiano, people grew old without having known a fraction of the experience that had already been Giacomo's in his seventeen years. He had been to Constantinople and Corfu, getting into fights and playing the hero everywhere he went.

When he told me his parents were actors, I began to wonder whether he hadn't just made it all up, but he always seemed in earnest, especially when speaking of his mother, Zanetta.

One day he told me how she had abandoned him as a toddler to pursue a career on the stage in London, where she was impregnated by the Prince of Wales. Whatever the truth of it, Giacomo became emotional. He loved her and he hated her;

that much was clear. His mother had sullied the family name, and the boy had made it his purpose to restore its luster. He set his cap at becoming a diplomat, following in the footsteps of forebears who, in the past three centuries, had served a succession of grand figures, among whose names I recognized King Alfonso II of Spain, Cardinal Pompeo Colonna, and Christopher Columbus. He wanted a part in history, one to equal his ancestors', however unlikely it seemed for the son of two actors. He had already taken his first steps in the home of the renowned Senator Malipiero on the Canal Grande, where he had grown accustomed to the company of the powerful and illustrious. He spoke of his ambition with a fervor approaching ruthlessness, sometimes scaring me, sometimes filling me with envy, though I had little reason to imagine any future of mine outside a workhouse in Pordenone. Still, intermittently I felt threatened by his dream, though I couldn't have said why.

He described what lay before him as if it were a decisive battle in some great war. His preparations had been meticulous, and he knew just which positions to take. That winter he would make a number of important alliances in Venice and try to obtain an appointment with Venier, the Venetian ambassador to Turkey, whom he had known in Constantinople. As he told me all this, I suppose he saw a look of dismay spreading across my face. He apologized, saying that, of course, it was impossible for me to understand how ugly Venetians could be.

"The countess has told me everything of Venice. I happen to know exactly the trials a woman must undergo in that city, the constant struggle. And all that just to find a husband, something that happens quite naturally in any village you care to name. I can very well imagine what ordeals beset a man who would seek a position there."

He looked at me sweetly. For the first time since starting to unfold his plans, he was fully aware of my presence, and I felt a childish relief, as I had the time the overseer's dog came walking up the path after having been missing for a week. At the same time, I was overwhelmed by an unfamiliar desire that submerged all others. Yes, I thought, I want him to succeed. Giacomo could indeed rise above himself. That has been ordained from on high. I had never been so convinced of anything. In that instant I would have given up everything for his success and happiness.

Then he told me of the night, when he was a child, that his grandmother had taken him to the island of Murano to see the witch who stopped his bleeding. And of the night that followed when he was visited by a fairy, of whom—he said— I reminded him.

Many times during those weeks I asked myself, Why would a young man like him waste the day in my company? Don't misunderstand me: In his presence I felt more beautiful than I ever had or would. I imagined myself clever and vivacious, never more than when I made him laugh. And yet alone in my bed at the end of the day, I was always afraid that he would come to his senses that night and not bother even to summon me the following morning. But once I had finally fretted myself to sleep, I sank back into the deep bliss our time to that moment had given me.

ONE MORNING he rang earlier than usual. It was hardly light. I threw on some clothes. My hair was still down, but I ran to him eagerly, elated as ever. I had scarcely entered his room when I realized something was terribly wrong. His face was completely unfamiliar, pallid with misery, and he seemed terribly upset. He allowed that he hadn't slept.

"There is something I am obliged to tell you," he said. "A terrible thing to be forced to admit, but I hope that by doing so I shall win your good opinion of me."

"If the pursuit of that prize leaves you so wretched, I'd beg

you to aim a bit lower," I said, trying to make light of the unimaginable thing that was filling me with such dread. "And tell
me why are you talking to me as if I were a lady, when yesterday
we were such good friends? What have I done, Signor Abbé? Let
me go fetch your breakfast, and once you've had it you'll be in a
better frame of mind to tell me the whole story."

I don't know how I found the kitchen or made it back with a
full tray and a jug of scalding water. My knees were trembling. I
poured his cup, and as he drank it silently I tidied the room and
closed the door to keep out drafts. Then I got into bed with him;
he let me snuggle up close. I was hoping that this familiar custom
might dispel the strange spirit that had entered our happy room.

He must have practiced what he was to say. He pursued
methodical argument with measured rhetoric and spoke for at
least fifteen minutes. But the effort was lost on me. I'd never
been one to think with my head; it simply wasn't my nature. I
knew only what I felt. And so what he presented as irresistible
logic, though I'm sure it was quite sound, I heard as folly. Only
one comment seemed important.

"I'm in love with you." So much flourish, only to come to
such a simple thing? "And loving you as I do, I can no longer be
confident of my behaving honorably. And that is why we must
see each other no more."

I stared at him blankly, as if he were speaking in Arabic. Was
this the way gentlefolk went about reasoning?

I am thirsty so I will not drink.

I am famished so I must fast.

I knew that in Udine there was a house where people with
such thoughts were strapped down on a wooden bench until
they thought better.

Still, Giacomo seemed not to have taken leave of his senses.
Moved to the point of tears, he described the horrors that
awaited us if we continued our friendship. Until then he had

managed to master himself by resorting to the saving remedy of schoolboys, to which, he said, he had recourse several times a day since our first meeting. But these measures were now failing him, as they were bound to do, and he could no longer be assured of being able to preserve himself from defiling my honor.

My eagerness to absolve him in advance for that same misdeed seemed to make no difference. He began to weep. I dried his tears with the front of my chemise, but the view I allowed him in doing so only seemed to inflame his dilemma.

"You love me," I said, "and because of that you would banish me. I should wonder what you would do if you despised me." I was not far from tears myself now, but I forbore. "You have studied; I'm a simple girl. Still, I'm smarter than you. At least I know that love is no sickness except when lost. I would rather have you healthy without me than watch you pine away in my presence. But I still can't understand it. I will do as you say, but it won't be for my good—and, if you would permit me, it won't be for yours."

That seemed to touch him.

"Nature's arguments are so much stronger than reason's," he said, taking me in his arms.

"Please," I whispered, "think of some other way. This problem is not so unusual. We can find a way. You can count on Lucia."

An alternative must have proposed itself to him as we spent a blissful wordless interval with no hint of a problem in the air.

After an hour my mother came to tell me to get dressed for mass. I was able to leave my patient, as a healthy color had already returned to his cheeks.

FROM THAT DAY we would kiss for hours every morning and night, playing all the games that mouths could play. On reflection, I already had a healthy love of life, but now I had acquired an awe and respect for its power to grant something divine. We were insatiable, for the very reason that Giacomo restrained himself from doing what would have brought us both the deepest satisfaction and shame. In this he alone deserves credit. Heaven knows I did everything in my power to weaken his resolve, even suggesting that the fruit had already been plucked, whereupon he laid me down for an examination I wished would never end. It seemed impossible to deceive him, such was his acquaintance with the feminine.

In his embrace, I felt the odd union of perfect safety and unrestrained appetite. The more I opened myself up to him, and to desire for him, revealing my soul as well as my body, the more certain I was of his protection. Because I dared to trust him, I was able to lose myself completely. And so it must have been in those days that I first came to identify comfort with shameless indulgence; nothing has ever made me feel more fully.

WE WERE STILL in this heavenly state in October, when the countess was to return to Venice in the company of those guests who had extended their stay at Pasiano.

We were inconsolable.

Giacomo declared his willingness to renounce all plans for his career. He had already composed a letter of apology to Senator Malipiero. I tore it up. He proposed to remain at Pasiano and work in the fields. I forbade it. This was no self-sacrifice on my part. I have never felt any admiration for such heroics. Indeed, I was moved by self-interest. My own happiness now depended on his. And there would be none for such a man if he renounced his deepest ambitions. I wasn't unhappy. I had already surpassed any imaginable hopes for myself.

We agreed that he would return the following spring, after

the winter season in Venice, and that we would be affianced after Lent. The countess, who had been midwife to the frolicsome birth of our relations, was only too pleased to be godmother of our future happiness. Toward this end, she asked her husband, who was unwell and had temporarily postponed his own departure for Milan, to extend Monsieur de Pompignac's appointment. With his work accomplished and Adriana's wedding behind him, the teacher had already packed his bags when he received the happy news that his employment at idyllic Pasiano was to be extended. He seemed quite confident of being able to manage a rather different sort of instruction with his new charge: In the coming autumn and winter, the countess had ordered, he was to school me in the manners of gentlefolk and make of me a wife befitting a diplomat. With everyone's happy assent and the countess's gracious patronage, next summer Pasiano would be the scene of another wedding.

Even on the eve of our farewell, with our future mapped out before us, and despite longings more intense than I had ever before known, I was unable to tempt the man who'd become guardian of my heart and my soul. Instead, we wept joyfully, holding each other until morning and pledging ourselves to each other in this life and the next.

As I stood waving farewell to the carriages, the elderly count standing beside me began to sniff the air theatrically, as one might having caught a first whiff of something on fire nearby.

"You're nice and ripe," he said. "I can smell it. I've learned that over the years. Nothing like that briny smell." He filled his lungs greedily. "You can always tell when a girl's ready for it."

I ran through the gate and down the road all the way to Pozzo, farther and farther, until they had all disappeared from sight and even the dust had settled.

7

"WHY SHOULD A MIRACLE be any less miraculous just because someone else can't see it?"

The Chevalier de Seingalt was still standing before my door, lost in thought and heedless of the cold Dutch drizzle. His wig was getting wet. Dark patches bloomed on his expensive silk jacket. The memory of the girl who'd once held up a glass and wondered at the changing shape of water had upset him.

"You know, we even promised to be eternally faithful to each other," he said suddenly, as if waking from a dream. "She promised to wait for me. But when I came looking for her, not six months later, she had disappeared."

"Perhaps there was a good reason."

"Indeed there was," he said, bowing goodbye again. "She was a woman."

II

A Great Imperfection

*N*ot far from Pasiano, on the bank of the Livenza, an ancient hermit lived in a wine butt. Sometimes my mother sent me there with a jug of milk or some leftover bread. The old man had spent his whole life fasting and praying, mercilessly flagellating himself and abjuring all worldly pleasures, all in the hope that, just once before he died, he might in imitation of Christ manage to perform the miracle of walking on the water. This was his only ambition, and he practiced every day from early in the morning until late at night. In front of his hovel there were always a few habits hung out to dry.

Then, one day, I arrived to find his clothesline empty. The old man was sitting on the ground in front of his barrel, tucking into roast lamb and a bottle of Lambrusco.

"I've done it!" he told me. "Last night the Savior appeared to me. He stood right there on the opposite bank and waved for me to come over. He wanted to see what I had dedicated my whole life to doing. The moment of truth had arrived, and I was full of fear.

"Then I stepped, very carefully, out onto the water, and behold! I stayed aloft and dry. A true miracle. I could hardly believe it was happening; one step at a time, I reached the middle of the river. Jesus was so happy He clapped His hands!

That made me feel braver, and with a few big steps I reached Him on the opposite bank. I fell into His arms. 'This is what I've given my whole life for,' I sobbed, 'renouncing all worldly pleasures so that one day I would be able to walk from one side of the river to the other.'

"Christ's face clouded over with pity. 'Oh,' said the Savior, 'what a waste! Just a few hundred yards downstream, there's a ferry.'"

The world is full of people who spend their entire lives seeking the miracle of love without ever seeing it. It's actually very simple and self-evident, except to those who seek it.

One need only have a different way of seeing things.

That is not something you can teach people. All you can do is tell your story.

I

I DIDN'T CRY. Sometimes I've regretted that. After seeing Giacomo disappear into the hills of Pasiano, I didn't shed a tear. It would have been a sweet sorrow, of such girlish intensity: a deep desire to lie down and die, an anguish that banishes everything else, as absolute as the euphoria that would have come over me a moment later, contemplating our eventual reunion. I could have sobbed all the air out of my lungs, directing my fury at fate instead of at myself. I would have woken the next morning invigorated, maybe even forearmed. Later, of course! Later, even the thought of my beloved's palm pressed against the rear window of the coach in mute farewell would be enough to break me, but by then death would have already passed me by, without offering a hand by way of escape.

Giacomo's departure was immediately followed by a period of such frenzied activity that I simply had no time for sorrow. That same afternoon, Adriana's tutor came into the room on the garden while I was stripping my darling's bed. Although clearly taken aback by my greasy hair and hitched-up skirt, Monsieur de Pompignac composed himself and declared that he expected me in the library at ten o'clock the next morning. He then asked me to put one of my feet up on the bed. Scarcely believing his eyes, he inspected my calluses and left with sagging shoulders.

I wore shoes to that first lesson. They were my mother's and too big for me, but Monsieur de Pompignac appreciated the gesture. He was more despairing than unfriendly. He paced around me like Madame de Maintenon's hairdresser circling a stray dog. He asked me questions, which I answered as I could. Now and then one of my replies would provoke a smile, although none seemed to bring him lasting cheer. Between questions he would parenthetically disclose bits of information that meant nothing to me. But not wanting to disappoint him, I kept up a friendly smile of my own.

Eventually he fell silent. He led me over to the window, took my face in his hands, and turned it so that it caught the light at several different angles. He sighed that at least my cheekbones were acceptable. Then he tried to send me off with Le Sage's adventures of Gil Blas in four leather-bound volumes, announcing that we would discuss it the next morning. I leafed through the books quickly but gave them back. I could read—that wasn't the problem—but not quickly and I told him there was no point in my even attempting something with so many difficult words. Monsieur Pompignac stared at me in sincere puzzlement. He browsed through one of the books as if to reassure himself that it really was printed in my own language and not in Aramaic. Then he relaxed. Slowly, as the full extent of my ignorance dawned on him, a smile appeared on his face. I was embarrassed and offered apologies he refused to accept.

"My whole life," he said, "I have struggled to make something of the debris that others have left behind. Filling gaps, plugging holes, repairing cracks, smoothing off rough edges. And now, just when I thought it was all over, for the first time I have been given a chance to show I can create a new form from a block of entirely unhewn marble. Mine, all mine, from the first blow of the chisel. It will be hard; it will hurt—of course it will—but what can one expect? Was Pygmalion daunted? We will shed tears of blood, you and I, but it is now or never!"

Hearing this, I wanted to abandon the effort, but he made me sit down and began opening books on the table before me. I read aloud from them the way I thought they should sound. He corrected me and explained exactly what they meant, over and over, until I started to recognize certain phrases and dared to guess at their meaning. We kept at it for hours. I grew hungry and thirsty. He called for water and some almond cake but wouldn't let me stop long enough to eat properly, so I had to gulp it down chunk by chunk, never pausing in my endless recitation of the conjugations.

When the sun had set at the end of that first day, Monsieur de Pompignac seemed no less exhausted than I.

Nevertheless, that night I didn't sleep.

I read.

Carefully I studied what we had studied earlier, line after line, and some lines still new to me. Then I tried to say them out loud. I remember the surprising thrill I felt when a word that had looked like so many hieroglyphics on the page suddenly came to life with a familiar sound after I had stuttered it out a few times. Although I hesitate to admit it because I could soon no longer imagine ever having been so foolish, I was nothing short of astonished to discover that all those symbols, even the many I could not yet decipher, in fact stood for things I had known for years. Uncovering this correspondence between the words and the world I knew was what finally dispelled the fear that books had always inspired in me. And with my fear I also shrugged off the cloak of mockery I had taken on whenever faced with writing and with people who always had their noses in books. The fear of which this cloak was made had not left me, but I had now found a new way of covering myself.

You can eat cake all your life without ever knowing what's in it, I thought, but you'll always need someone else to make it for you. Once you take the trouble to find out the ingredients, you'll be able to feed yourself.

The next morning I read the first page of *Gil Blas* to Monsieur de Pompignac. A new sort of smile started to spread over his face.

"Ma Galathée!" he whispered.

He hauled himself up out of his chair, took my hand, and kissed it. No one had ever done that before.

NOBODY COULD HAVE anticipated the success that followed. Studying seemed to suit me. Keen to please my teacher, I exploited this unsuspected talent to the fullest and hardly showed my face out of doors—much to the avowed regret of the stable boys and L'Aigle, the courier. (Around this time L'Aigle was thrashed and sent off for molesting a kitchen maid, apparently in a sulk over my having rejected him.) At night I kept myself awake over my books by anticipating my elderly tutor's delight the following morning. Once aroused, my hunger for learning was insatiable. After Count Antonio relieved me of my domestic duties—in exchange for a kiss— I was able to dedicate myself to my lessons all day. But that freedom hardly diminished the effort I made at night while the rest of the house slept. It was as if I were some sort of moth, using the bare months of the year to develop so I might live fully when the buds reappeared on the trees. The diploma held out to the students of Bologna scarcely seemed any carrot at all compared with the thought of Giacomo's astonishment at recognizing in me an intellectual equal when he returned in the spring.

From Le Sage's *Gil Blas,* my teacher led me to the adventures of Manon Lescaut and into the minds of many of the greatest thinkers of our age. They had struggled to liberate themselves from the bondage of sentiment, just as I was trying to rise above my own natural state. Their rule of reason appealed to me. I discovered it painstakingly as they did and, like them, came to appreciate reason as an instrument of unequaled power.

Monsieur de Pompignac had more than exceeded his commission and could have left well enough alone, passing our sessions together idly. But, inspired by his own success, he set his mark ever higher as I proved myself equal to the one before. In just a few days he began giving his lessons partly in French. My knowledge of that tongue was rudimentary, but he explained that it was the voice of science and of the very future of Europe. His confidence that I would master it was soon enough a prophecy fulfilled. Within two weeks I was able to reply in a suitably modified arrangement of his words, but once we had begun the painstaking journey through whole books of French, line by line, the words became my own. He seemed to have no end of offerings for me: Nani's *Histoire de Venise*, Fontenelle's *Mondes* and his *Dialogues des Morts*, Bossuet's treatises on world history, and Le Sueur's *Histoire de l'Église et de l'Empire*.

With the cultivation of my mind well under way, Monsieur de Pompignac was free to turn his attentions to more obvious though no less woeful shortcomings, first among them my posture. He directed me to sit like a marionette suspended by a single string attached to its ribs and he insisted that I always walk perfectly upright with short bouncy steps. To comply provoked more laughter in both of us than even my first attempt at the *plus-que-parfait*, but when it had become natural I noticed myself more at ease in the company of the gentlefolk of the house. This was also the effect of my tutor's having prepared a list of indelicate words that I was to stop using. As to permissible words, to improve my diction he made me recite the most awkward phrases imaginable with my mouth full of pebbles from the riverbed. Terrified I would swallow these and perish from their penetrating my liver, I cursed my tormentor and wept fruitlessly to arouse his pity. But in the end I profited; I was able to make myself understood without raising my voice, even with Monsieur de Pompignac standing on the far bank, the gurgling stream between us.

Some of the skills that he insisted were essential to proper bearing could at first not have seemed more obscure. There was, for example, what he called "enlarging the radius of projection of one's personality," a most recondite description of how to command attention in a busy market square simply by mastering one's breathing and adopting a tranquil, regal pose. I cannot exaggerate my astonishment on the first occasion of having applied this skill. Not to ignore the conduct proper at gaiety, my tutor took pains to teach me some simple dances such as the bourrée. We took meals together so I could learn to be at ease eating from a plate of my own instead of sharing the serving dish as we had done in my father's cottage. With this I was obliged to master the use of table implements. I told my tutor about my grandfather's custom of scooping up some polenta with just three fingers and, in the palm of his hand, shaping it into a little bowl, which he would fill with meat and gravy before folding it over on itself. He ate this way at the grandest of tables without spilling a drop of sauce, having practiced all his life to achieve such dexterity. In our region the skill commanded the respect of common folk, and I had always applied myself to achieving the same ease. I had, however, no choice but to take Monsieur de Pompignac at his word when he insisted that ease with a spoon and a fork was rated much more highly, though anyone could master that in the course of a single meal. To stir my enthusiasm he made me a gift of a traveling set of silver cutlery, taking the opportunity of my good humor to express a hope that soon I might also learn to contain my belching.

LIMITLESS NEW FIELDS opened up before me—page after page, book after book. It was dizzying; I was blind to all else. For as I luxuriated in this freedom like a foal put out in the meadow for the first time, I was too slow to notice my parents' growing unease as they observed me from behind the fence of their simplicity. Coming home at the end of the day, I did as I had always done, telling them everything I had seen and learned. But where once my talk was of familiar things from their own world—leaves that had started smoldering in the tobacco shed or an adder on the path—I now recounted how a nymph changed into a laurel to save herself from being ravaged or how a Corinthian queen took revenge on her husband by slaughtering their children. They tried to take it in and make it sensible ("Maybe that's better for the queen; now she might find a gentle husband who can give her new children") but soon they stopped trying and were reduced to smiles and nods. My enthusiasms pained them without my comprehending why. Eventually I tried to spare them by keeping mum about my new discoveries, but this only distressed them more when they came to imagine I thought them too simple to understand. For all my new cultivation I was quite unfeeling, little aware of the duty the learned have to accommodate themselves to the unschooled, who must be excused their shortcomings by their very nature.

In late November I noticed their spirits picking up. They were exulting over something, that was obvious, but wouldn't tell me what it was. On the first Sunday of Advent I awoke to find my parents beaming at my bedside. My father was holding something behind his back, which he handed to me after a brief, carefully practiced speech. It was the first book I would own. I removed the tissue paper and recognized it immediately: *Birth, Light, and Promise of Christ the Savior, Explained for the Holy Advent,* an essay by Fra Onofrio, our village priest. He had taken his simple thoughts on the subject—enough for a few rustic sermons—inflated them with borrowed Latinisms, random scientific argot, and meaningless flourishes, and bound the resulting effort in calfskin, an offering suitable for flogging among the parish worthies, who feared too much for their salvation to refuse. Less than a week before, he had palmed a copy off on Monsieur de Pompignac. Together we had laughed heartily at discovering so much bombast and stupidity in one volume. Now I was leafing through it again, under my parents' prideful eyes. I was overcome by repugnance for the greedy priest, who knew exactly how hard my father would have worked, how much he would have denied himself and his family to save up the price of this crudely gilded rubbish. The fact that Fra Onofrio had not guided him away from the foolish purchase proved the claim of Voltaire, whose work I had just begun reading, about the innate wickedness of the clergy. I turned the book over and over in my hands. I imagined myself taking the monstrosity back to our good shepherd and demanding the return of the money, but I elected for the sake of my parents to feign speechless gratitude. I'd repay this cost and more, I thought, once I was married to Giacomo and his career had begun. I hugged my mother and father and, fearing the charade would dissolve in tears, ran off, shouting that I had to show my prize to Monsieur de Pompignac immediately, though for my parents' sake I made certain he never saw the second copy of the priest's book.

For the first time I realized that I had traveled too far ever to find my way back home again.

81

· · ·

MONSIEUR DE POMPIGNAC must have noticed something in my mood, because he was unusually lenient that day. At dinner he chose the Fall as the subject of our daily discussion.

"Adam and Eve know it will cost them their innocence, and still they want to eat from the Tree of the Knowledge of Good and Evil. What sort of fool, Lucia, do you suppose would one need to be to renounce paradise?"

"Our ancestors had no concept of paradise until the moment it was denied them. In that sense it was wise to ignore God's prohibition. It taught them the value and beauty of the place they came from."

"Do you think this knowledge made them happier?"

"Surely you don't mean it would be better to remain ignorant of the good than to risk being parted from it—"

"—and realize you've squandered it. What do you think?"

"Absolutely not!" I exclaimed indignantly, for this was something he had just taught me. "Consciousness is our greatest gift!"

"So a difficult life with knowledge would be preferable to a carefree existence lived unmindfully."

"Knowledge consoles," I said. "In the contemplation of our grief at that lost paradise, our mind reduces the suffering."

"But wouldn't the wise man prefer never to have sorrows for the mind to relieve?"

"How would one ever know a paradise without having lost it? You make knowledge sound like a fault rather than an attainment."

"Knowledge makes us aware of what we lack. It *is* an attainment but, like every form of wealth, it robs us of our carelessness and innocence, just as it did the first man and woman." He paused here for a moment and then continued more gently. "I have reason to believe that you yourself have now felt this sorrow."

Was this the sight of my parents' hopeful faces as I leafed through the sad gift? "I've had an inkling of the tears you warned me about when you started teaching me."

"To acquire knowledge and reason is only the first step. Anyone given a chance can do as much. The greater test is the one that follows and defeats almost everyone: finding the courage to collect one's new belongings and depart, leaving others, even those most dear, farther and farther behind."

I nodded.

"This realization," he said solemnly, "is the diploma of our little course of study."

We would continue our discussion that evening not as pupil and master but as friends—and as friends who, at Monsieur de Pompignac's insistence, did not once deviate from the French.

IN A VERY SHORT time my life at Pasiano had changed radically. I no longer visited the forests or fields that had once nurtured my soul, finding my freedom now in the manor house, where my passage was so unrestricted that I could well have forgotten I didn't belong there.

One day Count Antonio joined me in the library. He demonstrated his interest in my studies by pulling out a volume from a hidden collection. It was the lavishly illustrated *Histoire de Dom Bougre, Portier des Chartreux*. The old man came up behind me and put the book down on the table before me. With each page he turned he drew unbearably closer, until he'd pressed his body against mine. I tried to put him off, trusting that a demurral proffered in French would have to be honored.

"Not yet, perhaps?" was his amused reply. He opened the

book at a page showing a courtesan obliging an officer with her tongue. "You can learn to talk like a lady, but how do you think such women come to enjoy the comforts of manor houses and carriages?"

He stroked the engraving with his bloated fingers, as if joining the illustrated characters in their play.

"Look, a trick that brings in an easy three sequins," he said, quite casually. "Remember that. Maybe even five, if such credit is due."

I stood up and hurried off to my lesson. Glancing back from the door, I saw the nobleman, still bent over his art collection, indifferent to my departure.

AT THE START of February, Monsieur de Pompignac went off without telling me, interrupting our lessons for the first time. I spent the free days poring over the *Lettres persanes,* enjoying the experience of seeing very familiar things through the eyes of an outsider. I could not possibly have suspected that I would soon become one myself. Four days later my tutor returned, looking run-down but with a self-satisfied smile as his gig, full of festive packages, drove up to the house. He had a surprise he would keep to himself for three days, after which he could no longer contain it.

He had traveled to Venice and back, not directly but via Modena, in order not to interrupt our instruction any longer than necessary. This route allowed him to circumvent the nine-day quarantine that the Serenissima had imposed, officially for sanitary reasons but in reality to force the recalcitrant council of Friuli into submission.

"Be that as it may"—he laughed—"the whole venture was for you. Voilà!" He handed me a pasteboard box with an enormous rosette and beamed at me as I opened it. It contained a long dress of dark-blue velvet. "Beauty like yours needs no embellishment, but when one reaches into a fruit bowl one can't help choosing the pear with the pretty leaf." It was the most gorgeous garment I had ever seen. I don't remember what exactly I thought—whether I was meant to clean the dress, keep it for someone, or iron it. De Pompignac repeated that it was a gift for me, but to wear something so precious was almost incomprehensible. Once it had sunk in, I pushed the dress away in fright, almost as if he had made an indecent proposition.

"I am far from being what you are trying to make of me," I said, "and I can't present myself as other than I am."

"Have faith in my hope. If it's premature, we'll know soon enough," he reassured me. "Count Antonio is giving a party for Carnival. You will be an honored guest. It's all been arranged. Unbeknownst to you, my dear, the old gentleman admires you and has taken a great interest in the progress of your studies. Don't say a word. All the dignitaries of the department have been invited; it would be out of the question to decline." Then he produced the rest of my new wardrobe, piece by piece, as elated as if the gifts had been for him. "Shoes, ankle boots—aren't they lovely?—gloves, silk chemise—feel it, just feel it!—a petticoat, and a corset—all new!"

When he saw me downcast at the prospect of a public examination, he laid all the finery down and came to sit beside me.

"There's nothing to worry about, *ma Galathée*! No one will know it's you." At the last he presented a mask, made of leather as was then fashionable during Carnival. "I shall introduce you as my niece." He glowed with anticipation. *"Je vous présente ma nièce, Galathée de Pompignac!"*

"You put too much hope in me, monsieur."

"We shall see." He laughed again and gave me an avuncular kiss on each cheek.

. . .

WE SAW NONE of what was coming.

The next morning Pompignac didn't appear for my lesson at the usual time. In the night his throat had begun to swell, and he remained in bed. By the end of the day the fever had come, and on the second day, as feared, his mouth and tongue were covered with blisters. These were the signs of a large pustule in his lung. The apothecary attributed the infection to the old man's foolish evasion of the Venetian quarantine. He did not expect a man of Pompignac's years to last more than two or three weeks at most.

I wanted to keep my "uncle" company, but my parents forbade it; the next day Monsieur de Pompignac was transferred to an outhouse on the edge of the estate. My father took his possessions from his room, piled them up in a field, and set fire to them. He wanted to throw the books onto the pile as well, but I stopped him. I told my father that the belief that the disease attached itself to paper was backward, a superstition dispelled by science. It was the first time I had challenged his sense with my new learning, an unthinking affront that obviously pained him. It was only after I had gathered up the unburned books and was carrying them away in my arms that I could feel a quiet sorrow that these people who had reared me with all their love had been made to obey my new authority as meekly as children.

Being ashamed, they would not deny me access to my teacher a second time. I was the only one to enter his room without fear. The servants left food and water on the threshold; I carried it in, sat down on his bed, and read aloud from the works that were most dear to him. Having taken it upon myself to nurse him, I adhered meticulously to all the precautions medicine dictated, disinfecting us both after each ministration. I wore a mask that had been drenched in alcohol, and I burned all his uneaten food as well as anything else he had touched. Fortified with the latest scientific insights, I tried to convince the others that there was nothing to fear, but it was no use. When his condition began deteriorating rapidly just a few days later, Fra Onofrio would administer extreme unction only through the window.

"What do you think, Lucia," Monsieur de Pompignac asked near the end, in a voice that suggested that he was still strong enough to argue the point, "who is better off, someone who dies unexpectedly or a condemned man who must count the days he has left?"

"They both lose the same," I said, "nothing more than today." My quip darkened his mood and seemed to plunge him into such deep thought that I blurted out, "After all, if I went walking in the mountains today, I could be crushed by a falling boulder."

"There is a significant difference," he said, in his calm, pedagogical way. "It surprises me that you don't see it. Imagine that you and I are standing under that boulder. You see it slipping and run away, skip off home. I see it too. It is hanging over my head. It wobbles. I see it tilting. I call out to you. 'It's going to fall!' And just then it slides free. I see it coming toward me. And all the while I am there waiting for it with my foot caught in a wolf trap."

I told him I was ashamed of myself, trying to be of comfort and yet having resorted to the kind of commonplace people use to disguise their impotence.

"It's nothing to brood about," my patient assured me. "Your emotions overcame your intellect. This proves that all the knowledge I have made to wash over you has not drowned your heart. Heart and mind, the necessary confluence for the greatest of human achievements. I couldn't be prouder."

I tried to feed him the honeyed pap that by then was all he could swallow. With the silver spoon he had given me, I ate some too, and we carried on as if this were just another of the many dinners we had shared.

He lay back and whispered contentedly, "*Mes félicitations,* Lucia. At last you've eaten a whole meal without once belching!"

THE COUNTESS OF MONTEREALE resolved to show her gratitude for Monsieur de Pompignac's contribution to her daughter's happiness by returning to Pasiano for his funeral. But as her carriage was delayed, his body lay unburied longer than the law allowed. Finally, in the dead of night, my patroness arrived. The next morning, to surprise her while also honoring my teacher's memory, I put on the dress he had given me. I combed my hair and put it up according to the fashion. Despite the sadness of the occasion, I was taken with my appearance; I swirled around a few times and practiced the curtsy I would use to greet the countess.

When I went into her room, the old lady was still in bed. At first she looked at me in bafflement, even after I had told her my name. It wasn't until I said something in my country dialect, and leaped onto her bed as I had always done before, that she was prepared to believe I really was her Lucia. I opened the shutters so she could see me properly and cuddled up next to her. For a few moments she was overcome as she struggled to take in the full extent of my metamorphosis.

Then her gaze fell to my face.

In an instant, all the contentment drained from her expression. She started screaming like a madwoman. My attempt to calm her by taking her hand had quite the opposite effect. Like a cornered animal, she fell back and pressed herself up against the wall, looking for some path of escape. She grabbed a handkerchief, poured eau de cologne over it, and held it up to her mouth, gesturing furiously for me to keep my distance. I still had no idea why my surprise welcome had so disturbed her.

The rebuff was too much to bear. I doubled over and fell sobbing to the floor. To see me so stricken softened her ferocity. Before fleeing the room, the countess paused to gaze at me crumpled on the floor. She was in tears, and for the first time since I'd greeted her, the tenderness I remembered subdued her wild fear.

"Dear child, poor child," she sobbed, "my darling girl, who will ever love you now?"

2

FAR TOO MUCH of our self-knowledge is derived from the gaze of others, which often we would sooner believe than the report of our own eyes.

When my mother, summoned by the countess, rushed into the room, I was still sobbing on the floor. Squatting before me, she took my head in her hands and studied a lump on my cheek. Her eyes were wild. In them I saw both pity and fear. Only then did I realize what calamity had come upon me.

Her eagerness to be far from me was more modest than the countess's, in proportion to her relative familiarity with what was unclean, I suppose; but the essential impulse was the same.

This time none of my rationalist objections could mollify my parents. Volume by volume, the library Monsieur de Pompignac had left me was consumed by the fire. Then my father fed the flames with the ball gown, scraps of blue velvet spiraling up on the smoke. Finally, when almost everything had been reduced to ash, they found the mask monsieur had bought for me in Venice and threw it on the coals. The smoldering leather produced the nauseating stench of the tannery. Dirty yellow smoke rose up through the eyeholes, while the cheeks and nose blistered and shriveled. With monsieur's gifts it seemed his plans for my future were being incinerated, and I was glad he hadn't lived to see it. Then I thought of my father and mother, who would have to watch my ruin. Could any particle of these decent people have felt justified in seeing it brought about by the very education that had drawn between us a curtain that could never be rent? After they had removed Monsieur de Pompignac's body and smoked the room with juniper, I was moved to that same house on the edge of the estate and laid on the same bed beside which for the last few days I had sat keeping vigil. I was finally calm. I closed my eyes, and in my feverish mind I saw Giacomo.

He was sitting beside me, pressing his hands against my cheeks and hushing me, whispering. Even this fantasy of his tender reassurances eased my misery. I calculated how long I would have to wait to feel his actual embrace. He was to return to Pasiano at Easter for our engagement. The disease had felled me several days before Carnival. My fate, then, would be decided in less than seven weeks.

Dispassionately I took account of the two possibilities: death and recovery. I could imagine both quite vividly; my imagination has always been very keen. This faculty that so often afflicts sensitive natures can also be a great source of strength. Such power can equally redouble one's suffering or prepare one to endure the worst.

For two days there was no change. In the night that followed, the pain struck, the pain of a thousand daggers. New lesions appeared on my upper arms. The disease was manifesting itself externally, which, taken together with my youth, improved my chance of survival, according to the apothecary. A third possibility—between death and escape—now occurred to me.

The thought was terrifying.

I asked to be bound. My parents didn't have the heart to do it. I begged them, and when they still hesitated, I cursed and raged at them as if they were obstinate servants, until they acceded to my demand. I lay on my back with my legs spread apart. My father lashed my feet with rope to the rails at the foot of the bed. My mother secured my wrists with a silk cord, which they passed under the bed and tightened with a cleat. I told them not to release me under any circumstances, no matter how wretchedly I begged, until I had recovered fully or—if it was God's will—had died.

In this position I waited.

Every hour brought new abscesses, while the old ones only seemed to swell.

After three days the pain suddenly subsided. For the first time I slept through the night, despite the awful stiffness of my muscles.

An itch woke me. It tickled up the inside of my thighs. It didn't worry me, and in my dreamy, drowsy state I felt it first as a pleasurable sensation. Then it spread outward: down my legs to the soles of my feet and in between my toes. I bent them. I spread them. I tugged at the ropes. They chafed but gave no relief. Then that same prickling began between my shoulder blades. I rubbed myself on the sheet as fiercely as I could, to no effect. The fire was now smoldering at the base of my throat and flickering between my breasts. From there it crept up to my nipples, where my skin was already swollen almost to the point of bursting by the accumulated fluids; there wasn't an inch of unmarked skin visible on the whole length of my trunk. I arched my back and jerked my shoulders but still gained no relief. Now the prickling flared up and began licking at my arms, my hands, and my fingers. I began to fear that unless I scratched myself somehow I would surely lose my mind.

The tingling behind my eyelids surprised me, for by this time so much of my body was ablaze that I'd become convinced my torment could not grow worse. Somehow it hadn't until that moment occurred to me that my face, the very reason I had ordered my parents to bind me, had so far been spared. When this awareness dawned, the taunting itch was quick to engulf my head. My panic fed it, and it spread over my body in new bursts. I realized my worst fears were about to come true. Forehead, lips, ears, chin, and cheeks, the worms of torment seemed to be squirming everywhere, even to the ends of my hair. They crept down my neck and wriggled out over all four of my limbs.

Hearing me scream, my mother came running. In the same solemn tone in which I had ordered her not to unbind me until the infection had run its course, I was now asking for release. The poor woman covered her ears as if the devil himself were tempting her. I forced myself to calm down to try a different approach. After speaking idly about something else for a moment, I allowed, rather offhandedly that my precautions at the outset of my confinement had been unnecessary, and might at this stage even worsen my condition. And so would she now, out of her abundant love, be so kind as to release me. This set her to doubting, I could tell. In my imagination I was already pulling myself free and exulting in relief as I clawed my wounds open. But I remained still and quiet to prove my point, smiling reassurances to my mother. She said nothing. She paced the room in indecision before approaching me and then as if having thought better of it turned away again. I turned into a demon. I vomited such a torrent of cruel filth out over her that she fled in tears without having freed me.

Now there was no hope that the fire would be extinguished.

DELIVERED UP to this torture and beset by fevers, I took the only escape I could see. The impulse was natural and beyond all doubt, like the urge to run from a burning house. I detached myself from my body and abandoned it. It was as if I had taken shelter in my soul, where for now I would hide, trembling in a corner.

At first I saw only the phantasms of delirium. They raged in devilry before my eyes, but I still preferred them to reality. Soon I could make out patterns in the midst of the whirlwind. Ideas coalesced, and I tried to seize on to them and organize them. After a while I could separate them out, one from another. I recognized childhood memories, former expectations and hopes, the terror of surrendering them, my desire for Giacomo, my grandfather's hands, the overseer's dogs, the lessons of good Monsieur de Pompignac. I was able to order it all according to the philosophers he and I had considered together, who were now coming to my aid for the first time.

By analyzing each new nightmare in this way, isolating each of its constituent elements, I was able to subdue it. Not without struggle—there were regular explosions of thought that threatened to overwhelm me. But each time my mind succeeded in mastering my emotions. And when it did, its triumph was mine.

I created order from chaos and, almost without noticing, gradually compiled the encyclopedia of my life, on a far smaller scale, of course, but in much the same spirit in which Diderot began. Each discrete element catalogued and put in its place, the odd bits assimilated in thoughtfully contrived rubrics. And when it was done, the fury subsided. I had snared the devil with my reason, just as sailors claim to catch the wind in a sailor's knot.

This was the turning point—and a revelation: If my reason could save me from this moment, there was nothing from which it could not deliver me. In this way my illness gained a meaning, and everything became subordinate to it. I resolved that, if I survived, I would let reason guide me for the rest of my life. It was after reaching this decision that I dared to abandon my fortress in the clouds and return to the ruins of my body.

The fever subsided.

The itch slowly died.

When I regained consciousness, I saw my parents at my bedside with Fra Onofrio's frightened face in the window behind them. From this safe distance, the priest was administering extreme unction. I thanked him and told him I would not require his offices.

My words had an astonishing effect. My father began to cry—something I had never seen before—my mother fell to her knees before me, and Onofrio turned white and ducked down under the windowsill. Apparently I had been dead to the world for three weeks, and having abandoned all hope they had released me from my restraints. They were awaiting my last breath when they heard me speak in a loud, clear voice.

From the garden Onofrio proclaimed my recovery an act of God, a divine intervention on this Palm Sunday and an indisputable miracle such as he had not seen in all the years of his priesthood. Doutbtless another pious disquisition was then born. I had a proclamation of my own in reply, to the effect that he was a fool and his God nothing more than an invention to explain the incomprehensible to the feebleminded, whereupon he fled and my mother crossed herself three times.

This much was true: I was cured and it was Palm Sunday! That gave me a full week to gather my strength before Giacomo arrived. I asked for broth and fruit and red meat. My appetite was back, and I feasted on all the things the others were denying themselves because of the Lenten fast. I drank as much as I could and gargled with malmsey to banish the evil taste from my mouth. This initial period of convalescence was so exhausting that I fell into a deep sleep after every meal, but every time I awoke feeling stronger.

On the morning of the third day I was ready. I wanted to test my legs and at long last to wash myself. My parents brought me washcloths and a jug of water, clean underclothes and a starched blouse, a hairbrush, soap, and lavender water. Finally, I asked for a mirror.

My father and mother exchanged a glance, and by the look in their eyes I knew everything.

MY PRECAUTIONS had saved my body from the worst. Bound throughout my frenzy, I had been unable to scratch and wound myself with my nails. Of the hundreds of pocks that had covered me from my throat to my toes, only a few had ulcerated. Here and there, I still had the scabs. My body would be left with small permanent marks in those places, but no other ravages of the ordeal.

That couldn't be said of my face.

My parents were reluctant to bring me a mirror so soon. To spare them unnecessary sorrow, I pretended that I was happy to wait. The moment they left, I pulled out my grandfather's pendant. It was small, but big enough. I saw myself through Santa Lucia's eyes.

The ropes that held me down had been unable to prevent me from thrashing around with my head. Furiously I had beaten my cheeks against the mattress, trying to tear open my eyelids, which were clotted with pus. Later my mother told me that they had tried to hold my head, which had swelled up by a third, and reduce the burning with wet rags. For a long time she sat behind me, trying to protect my face by clamping my head between her knees and her hands—to no avail. The itch was too intense, the torment too great. With the force of nature, I rubbed myself wherever I could—cheeks, forehead, ears, mouth, and nose—turning even the softest pillow and the finest sheet into instruments of self-mutilation.

After all these years, I still find it difficult to describe the ruin

I saw in that mirror. Suffice it to say that I didn't recognize myself. Taut red skin was growing over what must have been one large open wound. In time this new skin would heal, albeit unevenly, with deep craters and thick lumps. The left side of my face, however, was marked beyond repair by contracting scars.

Staring into the pendant, I was hypnotized by my reflection, unable to look through the glass, behind which, as always, even through this apparition, my grandfather's decorative artistry was glittering and shining in the sunlight.

GIACOMO ARRIVED EARLIER than expected, on Good Friday. I saw my love through the chinks of my closed shutters. He strode across the courtyard in his finest clothes, hurrying, elated.

I was fifteen, but eighty years would not have been time enough to acquire the wisdom for the decision I had to make. I had never left my home. I knew the world only from books. Beyond Pasiano, the only life I could imagine was that in Venice, and its merciless regard for beauty had been made all too vivid and clear, thanks to the countess. My "aunt" had hoped to strengthen me for the struggle that would await someone of my humble origins there, but with my illness everything had changed. I now heard her exhortations as warnings not to follow the path to what would have been my happiness.

In my disfigurement, I would be a leper in the city. And married to me, Giacomo would share that fate.

With this realization, I sank into a peculiar calm. Just days before, during my fever, I had clung desperately to reason, resolving it would be my compass ever after. Now I would invoke it again. I *was* aware of my emotions—dear God, how I was aware of them! My heart pounded, my soul was screaming, as I followed his steps across the courtyard from my gloomy hiding place behind the shutters.

The boy Giacomo had become a man and was much more handsome than I remembered him. If I hadn't fought against the urge with all my might, I would have run to him and thrown myself at his feet. I would have told him everything and begged him to take me as I was.

Instead, I smothered in my pillow several loud screams that came from the core of my being. Everything was raw inside. My emotions were ready to surrender to my reason. After this first shock, cool deliberation came as a comfort, just as the shock of the cold bath prepared for me after my sickness had made all the scars on my body contract and helped my skin to relax.

Giacomo was the personification of my happiness. If he chose to accept me despite my disfigurement, we could marry. I would be by my love for the rest of my life. This course, however, would require him to relinquish his ambitions. Our marriage would preclude any manner of career. This would be an unhappy fate for him, and in turn his unhappiness would be my torment. There would, then, be no hope for my own happiness. To follow my heart now would be the ruin of us both.

To defy emotion and free him to pursue his dreams: This was the other possibility. I would be wretchedly unhappy without him, but no more unhappy than to attend him in his misery. I could at least console myself with the knowledge of *his* happiness. He might mourn me for a while, but if he could be given to believe that I had betrayed him, his sorrow would at least be brief. He would grow angry and curse me, but in the end he would forget. That was my reasoning.

The first course produced two unhappy people; the second, only one. Ineluctable logic made the choice simple.

I acted like a machine, overruling my emotions and disowning them loudly three times.

As a child, I had once seen a peasant in Portobuffolè bitten by a poisonous adder. Shocked and helpless, I tried to reassure the man in a soothing voice, but he neither saw nor heard me. His veins had swollen and turned black. With perfect calm, he did what he had to do. He bound his thigh tightly, sawed his leg off below the knee, and cauterized the stump—all without a moment's hesitation.

With such assuredness and subdued emotion, I would have to act. I gave my mother the task of telling Giacomo that I had left Pasiano. Appalled at the idea of lying to the man whose love for me equaled her own, she refused.

Then I told her that today's lie would be true enough tomorrow. Giacomo would surely come back. It was impossible for me to stay.

If my fiancé asked what had become of my feelings for him, I said, she should tell him that they were entirely in the past; I had run off with the courier L'Aigle without so much as a mention of where we were going. There was absolutely no sense in his holding out any hope.

By the time she entered the room by the garden, which once again had been made ready for Giacomo, my mother's face was so tearful that Giacomo could not but accept the awful truth. It took him a full hour to recover after hearing it. He was served a pastry to fortify him and given some fruit and bread for the journey home.

IN THE MEANTIME, summoning reason, I requested an audience with Count Antonio. When he received me, I told him coolly that I had come to earn the five sequins, if his offer still stood. His astonishment was short-lived. The old man studied

my damaged face. For a moment I think he considered bar-
gaining but decided not to. He opened a drawer and laid the
money on the table. Then he leaned back in his chair, unbuttoned his trousers, and in a soft voice told me to undress slowly
before him.

I have never been a woman with an innate abhorrence of the
carnal, like so many who can bestir themselves to it only when
moved by a profound emotion. On the contrary. I am carnal by
nature. I knew at an early age that carnality would suit me. And
so the business before me was not so much an abject misfortune
as a logical necessity.

In the course of the transaction I realized that the pragma-
tism inspiring it was entirely in keeping with the new sense of
myself I needed to fashion. There would always be necessities,
but there would always be clear boundaries as well. To know
that was a comfort. Within these limits I could feel sure of
myself. And at that moment at least it was necessary not only to
secure my passage but also to know that I might still be desired,
however basely, despite my disfigurement; I had not been completely ruined as a woman.

I would have given anything to have discovered this pleasure
first with Giacomo, but I resigned myself to the way of things.
The old man mounted me awkwardly. Overjoyed to find that I
was still a virgin, he spent an eternity studying the phenomenon
at close hand, his fat fingers spreading me as wide as possible.
When he finally entered me, he clapped his hands like a giddy
child.

Even the coarsest man is no longer terrifying once in bed.
He can be hard and thoughtless on his feet, but his pleasure
overwhelms his capacity for calculation. With presence of mind
he can inflict pain deliberately, but any injury he inflicts reclin-
ing can have no cause but awkwardness. He becomes easy as a
child to please and, once pleased, as gratefully content.

I derived a certain satisfaction from the Count of Monte-reale's pleasure. I am not proud of it—it causes me neither pride nor shame to say so. Later, too, when I would please men who disgusted me—moronic, misshapen, or decrepit men—it was never without the hope that one day someone might do like-wise for me when I had the need to feel, if only for a moment, that I was beautiful and worthy of desire.

Under Count Antonio's sweating body, my mind once again came to my aid. Astonishingly I could look at that quivering, sal-low flesh and reddened face—and even smile at it—without actually seeing it. It did not appear before me again, even in my nightmares.

Imagination is the truest sanctuary.

There, and only there, I was together with Giacomo, that night and many others.

3

It was still dark when I left the house. I said no farewell to my parents, scared as I was that in their sorrow they would struggle to hold me captive. Their love had carried me this far. Now only my wits could take me farther. With Monsieur de Pompignac I had taken the first step. For the second, I had his words as guide: It was time for me to pick up my baggage and walk away from the world.

From the kitchen I took one of the wicker baskets the huntsmen used to carry pheasants. The wide straps permit one to bear quite a weight on the shoulders. Not that I had much to carry; I had hardly more clothes than I wore. I slipped unseen into the count's library and picked out several books that I had promised Monsieur de Pompignac to read one day. On impulse, I also plucked the *Histoire de Dom Bougre* from its secret hiding place. I had no claim to this valuable work, yet I felt no compunction, assured by my conscience that I had earned it. Perhaps I also hoped that the theft might compel the count to be more circumspect about forcing young girls to look at his erotic treasures. Certainly I knew these pictures were precious and might readily be sold to meet such needs as would surely arise.

Loaded with plunder, I took the road to Vilotta, reaching the village at first light. The peasants were already heading out to their fields. As most of them knew me, I hid in a ditch by the side of the road. Slowly I began to sense the gravity of the adventure that awaited me. I had only just left the farmlands of Pasiano, and already my legs felt leaden with misgivings. The straps of the basket were cutting into my back. For a moment I was afraid the sleep that had eluded me the previous night might overcome me now, but I resisted. An unknown strength growing inside me kept me wakeful. Despite want of both plan and purpose, I felt neither fear nor regret. On the contrary, I was filled with a strange joy. It seemed almost improper. I was leaving behind everything I knew. I had lost everything I loved, almost ashamed at exulting in such sorrows. Reckless but determined, I was giving up my life forever, with as much cold decision as I had yesterday given up Giacomo.

This unaccountable exuberance would stay with me for weeks, spurring me on at crucial moments. I headed south—mainly because the Alps seemed a pointless obstacle—reaching Rovigo first and then Ferrara. From there, after long wandering over the plain, I came to Bologna. All the time, my heart was overflowing. Life had shown its true face, and I was burning with excitement. We stood facing other like two rivals on the morning of a duel, menacing but well matched.

I liked Bologna. There were more people than I had ever seen in one place before, and it was easy for me to blend in. If someone started pointing, I would slip away between the women jostling in the market; if curious children followed me, I disappeared down one of the crowded lanes. Still, life was harder than in the country. Strangers had no qualms about remarking openly on my appearance.

Painful though that was, I would come to find what was said about me discreetly to be more hurtful. To find work in the city wasn't easy. There were beautiful girls everywhere with the same ambitions who were naturally to be preferred. I was forced to be more resourceful; trying harder to please, accepting less money and more abuse, I was never without means. Turning a blind eye to humiliation and pawing, I learned to accept what other women found intolerable, a skill that would later prove priceless. Still, my jobs never lasted long. Once, when I was serving in an eating house, someone shouted that my poxy mug was spoiling his appetite. Usually, though, the signs were more subtle. Customers who entered a shop having seen something appealing in the window would leave when they saw me. The daughters of the family I was serving as a charwoman were scared to come near. I was alert to such developments and eventually, rather than wait to be dismissed, I would move on. It's hard now to believe that I didn't lose heart completely. When you are as young as I was, I suppose even the most dismal failure urges you onward, and so I persevered somehow.

After several months, I found a married couple, the Morandi Manzolinis, who were remarkably indifferent to my appearance and allowed me to work in their household in exchange for food and lodging. He was attached to the Accademia delle Scienze, where he taught anatomy. As he couldn't bear the sight of blood, his wife, Anna, did the dissections for him. She produced exact wax models of the skulls she opened and the organs she removed, and it was these replicas her husband used for his lectures. She also pursued her own research. In the daytime I cooked and kept house—things she had no talent for—and at night I was free to study. The Morandi Manzolinis had no objection to my reading, and after a while they even granted me access to their library. When they had guests, I was allowed to engage help. They gave me a large sum of money to spend as I saw fit on the preparations for the feast. Penniless as I was, I could easily have cheated them.

"How can anyone be proven worthy of trust who has not first been given trust?" the signora explained, when she noticed my surprise at her apparent lack of worldly suspicion. "It's a gift few will disdain when offered it." This set her off on a more general lament of popular misconceptions that owe their persistence to the primacy of men in society. "The new scientific discoveries will finally put an end to this," she allowed, "by challenging male and female intellects equally." I took her convictions to heart and for my part never again brought matters of household management to her attention.

Most of the Morandi Manzolinis' visitors were like-minded. They were all of the best families, and I wondered how lives of such ease could have so inflamed the notion that women were diminished by trusting to their emotions and that only by the triumph of their intellects over their intuitions might they be truly free. They seemed quite free to do as they pleased, even in the sway of feeling, I thought. I never joined in their discussions, though they were quite insistent about seeking my opinion, as if to prove a point. I thought. it improper to embarrass a servant in this way and tried tactfully to refuse. They preached that the days of masters and servants were numbered and claimed that the world would soon be divided instead into the learned and the ignorant, the ultimate inequality, tolerable because anyone could erase it through study.

I preferred to hide in the library during these discussions, though I admit my own tuition had inclined me toward finding their optimism infectious. Even when I disagreed with them, I thrilled to the expectant atmosphere. In such a climate, it did not seem unreasonable that even my life might take a better turn.

This hopefulness among the women of the city had no more exalted patron than Prospero Lambertini, the former archbishop of Bologna and a cousin of Signora Morandi, who in those years sat upon the papal throne as Benedict XIV. He enriched the university on the condition that it employ female scientists and recognize "female knowledge and learning." The Holy Father had gone so far as to promise chairs to several of the femmes savantes, including my mistress, Anna Morandi Manzolini, and her dearest friend, Laura Bassi. It was, according to the signora, proof that faith in reason had supplanted belief in the spirit, even in Rome. Meanwhile, a papal commission, together with a delegation of learned women, strove for official recognition by civil and academic authorities of "female intelligence and intellectual capacities." One day a late lunch was served after the commission had drafted a petition that would be submitted to all academic institutions. Learned women had come from all over Europe to the Morandi Manzolini residence for this occasion; I served them sardines.

I had never seen so many guests at one time in my months of service at the house. I was uneasy but thought of my poor mother, who at Pasiano had sometimes cared for ten times as many. She, however, had achieved her competence through experience. The Morandi Manzolinis had confused my learning with maturity and burdened me beyond my capacity. Even having engaged a staff of twelve for the whole week, I scarcely had a moment to myself. I was surprised to discover that to give orders to others required courage and self-assurance, qualities that—despite the loving encouragement of my parents—had been shattered by the coarse taunts hurled at me in the streets. What little self-possession survived dissolved when a handsome student spent several days courting me. The effort had been an elaborate joke, he finally confessed in front of all the friends who had merrily put him up to it.

The trust of Signora Morandi came as my salvation, and I was determined, as she would have predicted, to prove it well placed. At first I lorded it over my twelve subordinates most theatrically, the way an actor plays a king, with a booming voice and borrowed grand gestures, but gradually I noticed what I should have known from my own experience in their place: They were more attentive when I spoke to them plainly and honestly, occasionally letting them catch a glimpse of my doubts. In the face of my ugliness, this goodwill, not lordly manners, was the key to winning their esteem and, in fact, to regaining my own as well.

I had been instructed to treat all the guests without regard to rank or title. As the signora explained, "They are all equally wise, and wisdom is the new nobility!" There would be no call to challenge the theory, as all in attendance were wellborn, women with names like Zenobia and Uranie, Alkmene, Celymene, Cleanthe, and Anamandra. I was overwhelmed by the strange sounds. They would call the roll before the day's deliberations got under way, and as I listened and served them coffee, I felt the same childish delight as when I heard the names of the fairies and witches in my father's bedtime stories.

Their days were long. In the mornings each in turn would hold forth, lecturing the others on her field of expertise, while the evenings were given over to less formal analysis of their passions and lives. In between they ate together. Near the sideboard, from behind a screen with a small window in it, I oversaw the table service. Some spoke Latin, but most were better understood in French. Every day they discussed recent discoveries; where experimental verification was possible, they regularly set out the necessary flasks, alembics, and retorts. Fascinated though I was, it was not my place to ask questions about these abstruse matters, and so my thoughts wandered, at times to the guests themselves: their expressions and the way they reacted to things.

Only one of them ever spotted me behind the screen. One day she caught my eye and held it with a commanding yet friendly stare. She was a French countess and stood out a bit even in that group. Although she was as well dressed as the others, as beautiful and as eloquent, she seemed somehow excluded from full membership in their coterie. She answered questions with unfailing good nature but never broached any new subjects. The effect of her bright-red hair, worn in a wide crown that required her to hold her neck straight and her head slightly back, was elegant and arrogant at once. I had heard her name a few times, but behind the screen I was so startled by her gaze that I couldn't recall it. She was staring with a restless yearning beyond my comprehension. For a moment I thought she might have been crying. Her eyes were moist and gleaming. But her expression was otherwise strong and prideful.

Though it was perfectly proper for me to be watching over things, I felt myself caught in some illicit act. I surveyed the table for a moment longer, as if no glances had been exchanged, then waved for one of the servants to take my place and quickly withdrew, taking refuge in the company of my signora's books. I stayed hidden away in the library until after the guests had gone to bed and the tables were cleared. Not reading, I sat motionless among the medical, surgical, philosophical, and astrological treatises, surrounded by Signora Morandi's scientific instruments and her wax models of body parts, arranged according to function. On the high shelves all around me were tomes wherein every known plant and animal species was described and illustrated, as were all known minerals and elements according to their properties and origins; even the earth itself— with its continents and oceans, its towns and cities and the roads leading to them—was documented in some thirty atlases.

The profound peace I feel in libraries goes beyond silence. The paper doesn't just muffle sound but stills the roar of my thoughts. I imagine the inexhaustible knowledge on the bookshelves and it consoles me. It is more than could ever fit into my brain, and this awareness calms me, for it reminds me I can never hope to know and understand everything. And with so much of it having been written down, the burden is lightened; the world has been classified, recorded. The facts, if I ever need them, are there to be found. In this way things written down are easier to let go of. Perhaps that is the purpose of all these books: Having taken account of the outside world in the most minute detail, they liberate one to discover one's inner world, which no one else can know.

I began to make a mental map of my feelings, to trace the path I had followed. It had been a year since I left Pasiano. In that time I had been forced to travel the farthest reaches of my emotional world, places where the climate fluctuated wildly. Sometimes I had to wade through poisoned lakes where all life was paralyzed as if by jellyfish. I had crossed deserts like a skittish blinkered horse, with my eyes fixed on points straight ahead. Only by constant forward-looking was I able to cross peaks and climb up out of canyons without losing my mind or abandoning hope—often I was simply unaware of the precipice I was skirting. That is why I hadn't shed a tear since leaving. Now, for the first time, I could pause and consider the road behind me. What had been strange now seemed familiar. Having come so far from my sorrow, I finally dared to stop and gather my bearings.

Wandering through my emotions in this way, I fell into a deep sleep. I awoke to find myself looking into the eyes of the French countess, who was bending over me with one leg astride the couch on which I lay.

"Forgive me, girl, I am studying your face," she said. "What was it, the smallpox?"

She towered over me. I was trapped and tried to sink into the cushions. Her head looked pale under the hair that swelled and bulged, big and fiery like the setting sun. Still leaning over me, she moved from left to right and back again, assessing the lay of the land.

"It hurts now, but you'll be glad of it later. Beauty is a dungeon in which we languish. You've escaped it. For now, that insight is of no use. Later, you will discover it yourself. When you do, think back on the woman who first told you so." With this, her curiosity seemed satisfied. She dismounted and turned away, as if having lost all interest in me. For a while she shuffled along the walls, studying the books. Now and then she picked one out and leafed through it. Finally, she ascended the wooden ladder, plucked a folio volume from one of the top shelves, and sat down to read, crossing her legs and hitching up her skirts like a peasant girl in a hayloft. This was so improper that I thought she must have forgotten about me entirely. To avoid embarrassing her, I quietly gathered a book from the table and started to creep away.

"You read?" she asked.

"When I find the time."

"A perfect example. You're a servant, so I immediately assumed you couldn't read." She rose to her feet. "Do you see how any of us can be misled by appearance?"

"Perhaps that is why beauty is such an advantage, my lady."

"In fact it is not. If one sees something beautiful, one assumes it's finished. That satisfies us. We look no further. We don't set to work. We don't dare cut it open, look beneath the surface. If rough diamonds were pleasant to the eye, it would never have occurred to anyone to cut the stone."

"Very kind of you to say so, my lady," I said, restraining my indignation. "For someone who is so blessedly free of it, you have a most profound understanding of ugliness." I tried to leave but she blocked my path. She took the book from my hands, noting with surprise and approval that the spine was in French.

"Descartes!" She stepped back for another look, then cast her eyes about as if to make sure that no one was playing a joke on her. Then, with a wry smile, she said, "Tell me now in earnest, where did Signora Morandi unearth you?" She took my hand and shook it, as if one gentleman were greeting another. "I'm Zélide. And you?"

Her bluntness about my disfigurement did not incline me to openness. The last thing I wanted was to tell her my real name. Girls called Lucia were as common in that area as flies around a horse's tail. To tell her my name could only promote one of her little theories.

"My name is Galathée," I replied. Her mouth dropped open, but I insisted. "Galathée de Pompignac."

She immediately burst out laughing. I was furious. I pulled my hand back and tried to leave, but she barred my way, grabbing me by the wrists, kissing both my hands, oblivious to my discomfort.

"Well, Galathée de Pompignac, I needn't worry myself on your account, that's clear enough. You've already started to cut your own diamond. You're an absolute gem!" Then she kissed me again. On the cheek. The wrong one.

THE NEXT MORNING as I was serving breakfast, Zélide winked at me as if we were friends or conspirators. I suspected her of seeking advantage with the others through a display of her ease with the lower orders, and I ignored the overture completely. This seemed to upset her. She rose, not having touched her breakfast, and hurried out into the garden.

At ten o'clock, I brought the ladies cakes and fruit before taking up my post behind the screen so that I could listen to their discussion, as I did every morning. They spoke in turns on the subject of the day: the extraction of energy from water. Most had a clear opinion, but Zélide remained aloof, and when I hurried off to catch the market on the Piazza Malpighi before noon, she, in a most indecorous display, followed me into the kitchen. I picked up a basket; she picked up another and, despite the impropriety, insisted on carrying it herself. At the stalls she squeezed the fruit, weighed the meat in her hand, and discoursed expertly on the herbs. Her father, she allowed, had been a teacher at a provincial town, and he taught her everything, though it was not enough. I thought better of challenging her pretense to humble origins.

"I happen to be shamelessly inquisitive," she admitted, "about everything and everyone. Don't you agree that science is, above all, a heedless indiscretion? A morbid urge to know, even things you were never meant to discover, things that can only disturb the mind? Most people would account it worthwhile to investigate the properties of the natural elements, but apply the same scrutiny to them and they will chase you off their land."

Zélide had acquired her title by marrying the octogenarian Count of Montmorency. On burying him, she acquired the means to bring teachers from all across the continent to her home in Vincennes. Over the years, she had found the thirst for knowledge to be unquenchable.

"I have noticed," she remarked, after some further disclosures, "you seem engaged by our debates at the Morandi residence. Why do you never venture an opinion?"

"It is not to serve you opinions that I stand behind the screen, my lady. And just as well; I scarcely understand a word of what is said."

"Then you should ask us for clarification. If only others in our company could admit incomprehension, how much more fruitful our exchanges would be!"

"I am in too much awe of all that knowledge to speak up."

"Ah, if some of the others could follow that example! Speaking about something one does not understand is foolish; asking about it is wise. There would be no science at all but for the honest admission of ignorance. One can learn only what one doesn't know."

"And since I know far less than you"—I laughed—"that, I suppose, makes me the greater scholar."

"I LEAVE BOLOGNA tomorrow morning," Zélide said, as we returned to the house with our baskets full. "From here I go to Naples. There are some new excavations there. At the foot of Mount Vesuvius a number of ancient Roman villas have been exposed, perfectly intact. This is the heart of our epoch. At last, the ash that smothers us will be blown away. Everything is coming to the surface. Nothing will be left unexplained. This is the challenge of the century. And one's duty is to be in the legions of the discoverers. I shall be there, and I would invite you to accompany me."

"What possible use could I be? Are there no Neapolitan serving girls?"

"As my secretary, Galathée." She blushed, and I was charmed to note that the easy bearing she maintained with those learned women of high birth had failed her in my company.

"If you would take me in out of charity," I said cautiously, mystified by her enthusiasm for me, "or because you see sport in the furtherance of my education, then I must refuse the offer, madame."

"Dear girl, I am the only beneficiary of my charity. You will discover that soon enough. Your handwriting?" she asked. "Is it presentable? If it is, you could write my letters, the reports of my findings, descriptions of the specimens we discover en route. I would entrust you with such small but indispensable matters, not so different from service in a great house. But more." Looking at me, she became less officious. "I would have a friend. And who can say for certain which of us would learn more from the other?"

4

THE ATTRACTION OF RUINS is one whose explanation I shall
expect in the hereafter! What allure could there be about a heap
of rubble? Zélide insisted on stopping at every pile of stones she
saw on our way south. After circling one, she could sit down
beside it and meditate upon it for hours. Meanwhile, it was left
to me to measure the debris formation, sketch it, and mark its
precise location on the map. Back in the carriage, Zélide would
discourse on the splendor and significance of the structure
whose fragments we had just seen.

My grumbling indifference to grit and shards seemed to
amuse her and prompted her to expand on the glories of
antique architecture, lectures that lasted until we had stumbled
upon the next pile. Some days we would cover scarcely five or
six miles in this fashion, after which my evening at the inn
would be devoted to reconstructing her extemporaneous insights and writing them out neatly.

Somewhere near Pitigliano, a lump of cement set her to cal-
culating the span of an enormous hypothetical dome and the
counterthrust necessary to support it. No matter that we had
not eaten all day and had miles to go before reaching the next
village.

"There isn't any dome!" I insisted, growing short-tempered.

"But there could well have been," she said

"And *that* might once have been a delicious roast chicken," I said, pointing to the excrement some shepherd had left among the rubble, "but knowing what it was is of no use to me now."

She laughed as if I had said something utterly absurd, and I began to suspect why the learned women of Bologna had never fully embraced her. "If you show me a roast chicken, there's no more to be said about it. But if I see what remains of it, my mind is freed to expand on the possibilities. The swain who fouled this place may have eaten nothing more than a dry crust of bread, but in my imaginings of the past, I have set for him a feast."

Finally we reached Portici, where we were to spend the autumn on the Bay of Naples in a simple apartment placed at our disposal by a distant cousin of Zélide's late husband, Maria Amalia of Saxony, recently wed to the king of the Two Sicilies. While strolling in the fields surrounding the house her husband had built for their wedding, Maria Amalia had discovered a well down which the townspeople would lower themselves on ropes, to reemerge within a few hours, as she learned, with antique coins and pins. She persuaded her husband to hire an antiquary to investigate the well's bottom. He found a system of underground tunnels and several marble steps, which he uncovered and laid bare. It turned out to be the top of a Roman amphitheater.

By the time of our arrival, the amphitheater had been three-quarters excavated together with the outbuildings, the pit now descending sixty feet, down which one climbed by seven narrow ladders. Marcello Venuti, who, together with his brothers, oversaw the dig, proudly showed us their progress. With a wet sponge he wiped a wall of the amphitheater, and its inscription suddenly appeared, as new as the day the carver had dedicated to Hercules the city still buried underfoot. It was proof, Venuti said, that this city was among those the histories told us had been lost under a layer of ash following an eruption of Vesuvius sixteen centuries ago, soon after the death of Christ.

Zélide seemed deeply moved by this, especially as we walked the antique road around the theater, a road not so different from one of our own age. The Venuti brothers pointed out shops and small restaurants and the pots and dishes that still lay where they had been found. Bottles and cups on the counter gave the impression of a modern inn whose customers had just taken their leave. We were then brought to an adjoining basilica detectable from the outside only by recently exposed bronze doors. Some cool water was fetched for us, and we were left alone to ponder the sudden extinction of a world.

As my eyes adjusted to the gloom, the splendor around us became apparent. Looming up in the diffuse light from the small star-shaped opening in the otherwise buried cupola were two equestrian statues. Then I discovered the intricate, colorful patterns laid into the marble floor, glimmering golden figures in the mosaics on the walls, and, in the middle of the immense nave, an enormous porphyry basin filled with water and deep enough to bathe in. The earth was like an oven. The air hung heavy under the arches. Our cotton garments clung to our bodies. I dabbed my face and shoulders, cooled my wrists and ankles, drenched my parched hair. With the touch of cool water my mistress stirred from her reverie. She unbuttoned her blouse and leaned over the basin to wash her upper body, her red hair looking unreal in the light reflected on the water.

"Do you see, Galatea?" She sighed. "Everything already exists. Whole and completed. It exists, whether we're aware of it or not. Reality does not depend on our observation of it." She stretched and stood there for a moment with her arms aloft, trying to direct the faint subterranean draft across her damp body. "And just as the earth holds all its truths within it, so too do we carry all the answers within ourselves, even to questions we haven't thought to ask."

As exuberant as a little girl, she suddenly clasped my hands.

"Yes, dear child, I am convinced of it! Our minds today furiously seek out new knowledge but neglect the old. What place has reason made for innate understanding, the things we know beyond question but without a shred of evidence? Absolutely none! My learned friends have excluded themselves from knowing all but the little their eyes and ears can show them."

I disentangled myself from her grip and took up my notebook, knowing that this excited burst of insight would not excuse me from having to order these disjointed thoughts after dinner, by which time I would have the added difficulty of trying to remember them. Zélide's torrent of exuberance continued all the same.

"Reason is but the shell of consciousness, beneath which emotion is far more knowing. Only in our hearts, where no one can judge us fools, do we dare to trust and know everything without words. If we never had to meet the world without, we would never doubt our intuition for a moment. But go meet it we must, and, when we do, our vanity demands that our inner selves be as presentable as our dress. We comb our thoughts neatly and pleasingly. What child without the power of calculation does not know instinctively a good soul from a wicked one, or what she must do to be fed, to survive, and be loved? How much of what we seek to know, the answer to every great question, is given us at birth? We haven't forgotten merely how to search our souls for the answers but even that the answers are there to be found. We remain oblivious to it all, just like the millions who have trod this city's streets for centuries, never suspecting what lay just beneath their feet. Intuition is never stronger than when we are born, and it fades helplessly as we learn to think rather than feel, but we never lose it completely. It lies buried beneath the avalanche of argument and reasoning by which we believe we understand. Now and then, in the odd dream or wayward thought, we might suddenly rediscover it. An artist would call it inspiration; for a believer it is revelation. But for those who would call ourselves rationalists? Perhaps to us it is simply an idea, a moment of enlightenment in which appears the solution to a problem not yet formulated. The unexpected insight astonishes us. How proud we are to have learned to think as individuals, so proud that we can no longer bring ourselves to consider that we might once have been part of a greater whole. And I don't speak even about those moments everyone has experienced, the odd thought of someone just before you bump into him or the unexpected vision of a loved one, which you later discover occurred to you as that dear soul drew his last breath somewhere miles and miles away. These insights lie at our feet like shards. The obvious thing to do at such a time would be to dig deep within ourselves, but that's the one thing we don't do, because we can't grasp it with our intellect, and nowadays we're frightened of anything we're unable to explain rationally. Instead, we pick up our shard and slip it into our pocket in the hope that one day, by chance, we might discover another piece that fits. I tell you, Galatea, the noble scientific impulse has drawn a screen over our original knowledge. It buries what we know ever deeper under the accumulation of facts, until we can scarcely perceive what was once so plain."

The Venuti brothers must have caught more than a glimpse, arriving before Zélide and I had a chance to button up after bathing ourselves. They appeared in the sun-flooded opening in the bronze doors, but perhaps their eyes had not yet adjusted to the gloom as we hastened to gather up our hair and don our garments. Marcello had the scholarly pallor of one who has spent too much time underground, but Ridolfino and Filippo were both men in their prime, sunburned and sweaty from digging. They had rolled up their shirtsleeves and even the legs of their trousers, and mud was caked up to their thighs, with the hair on their legs plastered down like the fur of animals. Shamelessly, they stared at those still wet parts of my dress that revealed more of my body than anyone with a claim to decency would have allowed himself to observe.

Despite this brazen conduct, I was glad when they presented themselves freshly washed that evening, inviting us to attend with them the festivities of the feast of San Gennaro. Cheerfully they took us by the hand, leading us out onto the terrace, to show us the glow of fires lighting up the city on the other side of the bay, from the Castel dell'Ovo to Posilipo. But Zélide wouldn't be drawn out.

"Very well, then," I teased, "I shall enjoy the gentlemen's attentions undivided," but my mistress responded with a morose silence that made me feel I had misspoken. I offered to decline the invitation and spend that evening, like all our others, in reflection and transcription, but perhaps feeling a bit of guilt at having oppressed the gaiety of youth, she urged me to go off, saying she would take the time to order her thoughts solitarily for once.

THE NEAPOLITAN GIFT for celebration is unmatched, and it was almost dawn by the time I returned home, drunk with success. Neither Ridolfino nor Filippo seemed repelled in the slightest by my disfigurement, perhaps because their work had accustomed them to the sight of damage. Nor were the brothers embarrassed by each other's ardor. And so in their arms I knew a passion that might have frightened another girl my age. In truth, since my confinement, no man but the old count had looked upon me with desire, and before that my experiences had been limited to Giacomo's sweetly timid touch. On that feast of San Gennaro I abandoned myself completely to my yearnings and exerted myself in ways not to be found even in *Dom Bougres*. I felt the pleasure not in my body but in my soul, where the sensation was all the more intense. My soul seemed—I don't know how else to say it—elevated by my shamelessness to the point of having broken free from my body, free to look down from a great height at the contortions below. I was moved beyond all expectation by the feeling of being so hungrily wanted. Even then I knew it was possibly the only time I would ever arouse such great longing in two handsome young men, and to have satisfied them both produced a feeling of great contentment, an exalted peace of mind. And for a moment my imperfection was forgotten as I stopped thinking and only felt. After our play was over, there was not a thought in my head as I lay gazing at the relaxation and childish gratitude on the faces of the brothers, recovering from their exertions with their heads on my belly.

Zélide was asleep when I returned, but the oil lamp she had left burning still flickered on her writing table. Beside it lay the essay she had written while I was out dancing. I was so full of myself that I imagined she had left it there to be found as a mute reproach; in my drunkenness, I felt capable of waking her to have a row about her bloodless, joyless old spirit.

Fortunately, I set to reading the essay instead. It was full of echoes of our conversation in the basilica. Zélide elaborated her theory of the loss of intuitive knowledge with age, in a tone and with a force that made me feel banal and abject in the afterglow of lustful satiety. In every word, I recognized her painfully sensitive soul and its refusal to surrender to the inflexible regime of reason. She spoke from her heart, relying on her own experience, without referring to science or attempting a logical proof. It was one of her most inspired works. In a somewhat altered form, together with two later dissertations on the same subject, it would eventually be published in Nancy—under the pseudonym M. de M.—as *De l'origine du savoir.* I still have a copy. Another was added to the collection of the Bibliothèque du Roi on the recommendation of Monsieur Bignon of the Académie and can, to my knowledge, be consulted there to this day in the modern philosophy section.

The birds awoke as I sat reading. The sun came up. A sea breeze extinguished the oil lamp and carried the smell of ripe lemons in from the garden. My body and mind were so exhausted that they offered no resistance to ideas I would surely have contested otherwise. In my ecstatic state, I was scarcely able to distinguish the sensual delight still trembling within me from the passion of Zélide's words, although my weary head was mostly incapable of following them.

I did not go to bed. Long after I had finished reading, I remained seated at the table. I felt emptied. Even if my salvation had depended on it, I could not have got my body to move, and my mind was frozen in the same way. I sat there, without will or thought, staring out over the waves at the distant islands. Zélide came in and stood next to me without a word about the essay lying in front of me. She only laid a hand on my shoulder. I began to cry—for the first time, in fact, since fate had marked me. A bit of tenderness had achieved what the sorrow of a year and a half could not. I wept and wept. And Zélide and I stared out to sea mutely.

ZÉLIDE CONCLUDES her treatise *On the Origin of Knowledge* by comparing our innate but undiscovered knowledge to the buried cities around Vesuvius, whose existence we never suspect until the day we happen upon an ancient street and find ourselves walking on antique cobbles. Finally, she compares both to love, which likewise admits of no rational proof, but which—sometimes long after having been forgotten or given up as lost—always reemerges as an incontrovertible presence: *Each of us, after all, accounts himself capable of love, never doubting the capacity for a moment, even though the proof of it eludes us until the day we find someone who is worthy of this gift.*

"THAT'S ENOUGH NOW," said Zélide at last, drying my face. She ordered Turkish coffee and a hearty breakfast, which I couldn't bear the sight of; just the smell of freshly baked bread was enough to bring the gall churning up in my throat. "I have seen enough of Naples and will be returning to Paris. If you have no other plans, you may remain in my service."

As far as I knew, I had no plans at all, other than a firm resolution never to drink another drop of wine as long as I lived. I promised Zélide I would stay with her, although I imagined my blood was so badly poisoned that I might succumb that very day. She picked an orange in the garden and peeled it for me, despite my insistence that I would not be able to swallow a bite.

"I can think of nothing that would make me happier," she whispered shyly, "than to know that I can count on your friendship"—whereupon she hazarded the loss of it by forcing a segment of orange on me. She ordered the servants to close the shutters, fluffed up the cushions, and laid me down on the couch to rest. She dabbed my forehead with a cool cloth until the hammering began to subside.

"It's agreed then," she said. "You and I shall leave together for Paris. I'll write ahead telling them to prepare one of the rooms on the garden for you. There's plenty of time to get everything ready. On the way, we might spend some time in Venice."

I sat up cautiously, pressing my hands against my forehead as if by pressure I could dampen the pounding.

"Venice?"

"Yes"—she beamed—"six weeks or so, at the most. Or would you like to stay longer?"

5

A DEAD DOG, its gut bloated, was floating amid the cudweed. When the gondolier pushed the animal out of the way with his paddle to moor the boat, its skin burst open. Two pieces of hide stuck to the quayside. As we stepped ashore, they slapped against the stones under our feet.

When I first got to know Giacomo and tried to picture life with him in this city, my imagination had failed me. In snatches of the countess's conversations I had caught as a child, it seemed a place of mystery, an enormous open-air ballroom filled with ladies, thieves, and doges, singers and actresses, a playground I might hope to enter somehow when I was older. Maybe I saw color when I heard the name, lots of colors crowded together; I definitely saw people dancing and everywhere the glitter of sunlight, lamps on water, and enormous palaces covered with gold. Having never seen a Venetian palazzo, I imagined country homes like ours in Pasiano, but with their staircases and landings in the water, lined up and separated by beautiful parks. From the stories Giacomo told as I laid my head in his lap, my eyes shut tight, I mapped a world of my own with squares and quays we could walk along, arm in arm. The mansions in my mind's eye, while bearing no resemblance to real houses, had porticoes and courtyards that felt familiar and safe entirely because my love was at home there and had played in them as a child.

That association changed the moment I knew that I would never be his and his city would never be mine. I had not given San Marco or the Canal Grande another thought. I had reconciled myself never to visit the lagoon. And when, against my wishes, the places Giacomo had described returned to my mind, I pushed them aside. In the interim, darkness had taken the place of light; what had been radiant was now tarnished. Where the sun had shone through stained glass, only gray sky could now be seen, through panes the pigeons had fouled.

Compared with my fallen dream, the Venice I found with Zélide was far worse: sludge on the bridges, alleys choked with rubbish stirred by vermin, a smell everywhere of unbathed bodies. The stench of the fish market hung over the Rialto. On the steps were dead birds, their necks wrung by the maize vendors. Everywhere, screams and curses rose up from packed streets. The crowd knotted together in the *sottoporteghi*. Strangers elbowed past one another from every direction. In front of the churches, beggars importuned menacingly, gesturing with their festering stumps.

Zélide sighed. "Enchanting, the way the people here have made not the slightest concession to modern civilities! Fighting one's fellows for every breath of fresh air, one learns to appreciate life. Imagine that in the Tuileries!"

So charmed was she by all this earthiness that I feared she would lodge us at an inn full of tanners; thank God, she had already rented an apartment in the Palazzo Cini. As soon as we stepped through the door, the filthy city seemed to dissolve behind us. Thick walls muffled the cries, heavy curtains kept out the smoke and the stench, and in all the rooms an ingenious mechanism allowed one to admit a fresh sea breeze at the tug of a cord. Here I entrenched myself.

Once a day we crossed the canal to the Piazzetta to visit the library. Sometimes we took a boat to San Lazzaro to see the Indian miniatures and Egyptian manuscripts that are kept there under the guard of Armenian monks. Beyond this, I accompanied Zélide on short, purposeful excursions to places where I was certain not to cross Giacomo's path: the seamstress's workshop or the ladies' bathhouse, for instance. At the latter, I drew a peaceful breath. Zélide had chosen one not far from the Ghetto, in Cannaregio, which was mainly used by ordinary women from the neighborhood. A few times a week we hired an enclosed gondola to take us there and spent one or two hours enveloped in the warm mist, as an elderly Ottoman masseuse rubbed us with oils. On these precious afternoons we sat silently together, without a thought.

Generally we dined at home. When we received an invitation, or Zélide, wanting diversion, set out for the *ridotto,* I would contrive a reason to remain behind. When she entertained guests in the apartment, I typically claimed illness and took to my bed. Beyond the windows of my room, which were tall and narrow as those of a chapel, the city lay all about me, wreathed in blue haze or trembling in the dull glare of the sun, seeming always far enough away that I might comfort myself to imagine it a mirage or a phantom of a fever that would soon pass.

If I heard laughter on the water, I heard it as mocking my cowardice. When I heard a voice like his—and there were dozens of times every day when I thought the moment had come—I had to force myself not to rush to the window. Fighting back the pain in my soul, I pressed my nails into my flesh until I bled, but my resistance was futile. The more I struggled to extinguish feeling, the more vividly I imagined that somewhere out there, on the squares around the markets, lying among the peels and the rinds, some remnant of my happiness must have survived.

Just as I came to believe I would go mad if I did not leave the city immediately, I was delivered. The theaters reopened. When an elated Zélide came home with costumes for opening night and news of having rented a box at the Teatro Chrisostomo, I did not immediately recognize the solution that had fallen into my lap and begged off in my usual way; an event to which the grandest people of Venice would be drawn was almost certain to lead me into Giacomo's path. It wasn't until Zélide donned her tricornered hat that the form of my deliverance was made plain: For the whole of the theater season, from October until mid-December, it was the custom of the Venetians to go about their daily lives in masks. I could move as if invisible among them. I might even observe Giacomo from close by and be assured of the success of his career and his happiness.

Zélide, having no idea of the phantoms that had plagued me in the preceding weeks, delighted in the revival of my spirits. She wrapped me into the costume she had chosen, tied all the bows, and pinched my breasts until they flushed—just as I did for her when she was going out. She had chosen for me a *moretta,* a black leather mask that one held in place with a button between the teeth. I was afraid that, in my nervousness, I would let go the bit, betraying my true self. But Zélide, desperate to lure me out, thought nothing of exchanging masks, and so it was I wore the most beautiful one to be seen that night: a confection of white velvet, with small diamonds around the eyes. For me, however, its surpassing quality was that it covered the whole of my face and could be fastened to my hair securely enough to withstand the liveliest dancing.

I COULDN'T take my eyes off the crowd, both in the theater and milling about the entry hall. It seemed not a soul was following the performance—some divertissement about Marco

Polo, the hero of the republic who had been born on the site of this stage. The Countess of Montereale had not exaggerated the spirit of the place; it was plain even to me that everyone was far more concerned with securing or fortifying position for the season ahead than with Marco Polo's adventures. The interval was a particularly precious opportunity to draw attention to oneself with a conspicuous show of beauty or wealth or wit; failing these virtues, possession of a vicious rumor might equally arouse the interest of those who mattered and guarantee admission to all the imminent soirées. Inversely, a single faux pas or slip of the tongue was enough to negate whatever favor one had earned over the previous year. Outsiders imagine that Venetians wear masks in a playful spirit, but the truth could not be more deadly earnest. For all but the Doge himself, concealing one's identity is the only refuge, a respite from constant suffocating scrutiny. I do not exaggerate the gravity: A man who disgraces himself on the Rialto loses everything and can only choose suicide or exile. Pleading he has been mistaken for another, thanks to the mask he may preserve his life, even though suspicion alone will have shattered his reputation.

To see for myself the sovereignty of appearances in the city was in its way a comfort; I had been right to give up Giacomo. Our alliance would have ruined him. Never having wavered in this conviction, I became very curious about his career. The greater his success, I reasoned, the better justified my sacrifice. I might find comfort too in discovering he had done extremely well, a consolation for the sorrow of finding myself in this city.

That evening, however, there was no sign of him. I plucked up my courage and began to ask after the young Abbé Casanova. The name seemed unfamiliar to most and only three turned out to know him: One said that Giacomo had served for a time as a soldier at Fort Sant'Andrea; another thought he had gone to Rome to try his luck; according to the third, he was either on Corfu or in the hands of the Mufti of Constantinople, the Turkish pope. Of course, the uncertainty of all respondents gave me to believe I had learned nothing.

Then I saw Adriana! She was there with her husband and a few friends. I had already rushed up to her and was standing breathless before her, when I realized from her look of astonishment that she would have no way of understanding my enthusiastic approach unless I revealed my identity, which—if she still saw him regularly, as I devoutly hoped—she would then disclose to Giacomo. I elected to remain anonymous, exchange a few pleasantries, and ask as if by chance and with all possible nonchalance about the young abbé, whom I happened to know had been invited to her wedding. On hearing his name, she laughed a little, as if many before me had asked the same question. She had not seen Giacomo for some time but knew the whereabouts of his brother, Francesco, who was now studying theater architecture. He earned a living as an artist and had painted a number of murals of naval battles for her. Preserving the casual atmosphere, I bade her a sudden but cheerful goodbye, though I would gladly have given a year of my life to talk to her about poor Monsieur de Pompignac and reminisce about the summers in Pasiano, her dear mother, and my own parents.

THE NEXT MORNING I astonished Zélide by venturing out masked and alone at midday. I took the *traghetto* to the Church of San Samuele, behind which I had no trouble finding the large house where Giacomo had lost his father and that he had described so lovingly: the sculptured angel above the door, the Moresque staircase with steps that were much too high, at the top the marble lion's head whose mane had been worn down by the strokes of every passing hand. On the piano nobile was Francesco in his studio. One wall was covered with a large canvas, on which he had depicted the Battle of Lepanto. Scale models of stage sets he had designed were everywhere, along with innumerable walnut and rosewood models of the most ingenious landings and spiral staircases, some no larger than a thumb, others the size of a man. I found him sketching and eyed all his work thoughtfully, pretending to be a lady considering a commission. I asked about prices and ideas for a ceiling mural. I sounded quite convincing, I thought.

"You wouldn't perhaps be here to inquire about my brother, signorina?"

"What makes you think that?"

"Tintoretto was visited in his studio. When someone wants *me* to paint a ceiling, I am usually summoned to the house. If I'm not there within the hour, the work goes to someone else. My only visitors here are vile old usurers to whom I owe money and beautiful young women who ask about Giacomo. I don't believe I owe you money, so I am sorry to inform you that you are out of luck. He's gone abroad."

"You must have to put forth that story quite often."

He laughed. "It has the virtue of being true."

Francesco squinted, as if bringing a portraitist's eye to bear on me; his stare was so severe that I couldn't help but feel my mask to make sure it hadn't slipped.

"You must forgive me, signorina, but I am at a disadvantage. Perhaps I know you?" he asked.

"I don't think so."

"Something familiar. In your bearing maybe."

Francesco brought me a drink and then, with evident fraternal pride, produced a letter that he allowed me to read as he continued sketching. Giacomo had sent it recently from Turkey. The tone was laddish, very different from how I remembered him, and I found it not pleasant at all. He described the sleight of hand by which he'd managed to swindle a dragoman, how he'd taken to smoking a hookah with *zamanda* tobacco, how he was forbidden to set foot anywhere except in the company of a janissary, who showed him a harem and mocked his ignorance of the morals of Muslim women. It amused Giacomo that these women would sooner bare their bodies than their faces, the covering of which was prescribed by law.

I replaced the letter without reading it to the end.

"I assure you, that brother of mine loves to embellish. So determined is he to relish life that if a day passes without some extraordinary experience, he is likely to invent one. Don't take offense."

"No," I said. "Why should one take offense?"

Apparently Francesco was regularly called upon to give reports of his brother; though I took no pleasure in this impression, my need to know was strong. It seemed too that Giacomo's career was not progressing as splendidly as he might have wished. Still, for someone of humble origins, he had managed by dint of charm and erudition to gain the confidence of a number of influential people, both within the Republic and in the Vatican. The prospects for his return were favorable.

And love? I wanted to ask. Have his qualities helped him to make a good match? But having been identified at least in my motives, I couldn't inquire and instead stood up to leave.

"As to affairs of the heart . . . ?" Francesco offered, almost disappointed by my reticence. Without finishing his sentence, he laid his sketch down and turned it around so I could see it properly.

"Very skillful," I said. "Who is it meant to be?"

My dress, my hair, my posture were all perfectly rendered. He had drawn everything except my mask. In its place he had drawn my formerly unblemished face, the face he would have remembered from his visit to Pasiano and whose memory faded a bit in my mind each day. . . . I betrayed no emotion but studied the portrait politely and slid it away from me without showing further interest.

"And his loves?"

"He has them."

"I'm glad."

"A most immodest variety."

"Indeed," I said, turning away to escape the gaze that was still fixed on me. I stood close to the naval battle and feigned mesmeric attention.

"He nets them one after the other, and sometimes a brace at a time."

The waves were red with blood. The Turkish fleet was shattered. A commander was drowning between the oars of one of the Serenissima's triremes. His turban had come undone and trailed like a long golden ribbon on the water.

"Does it surprise you?" Francesco went on, now with evident malice.

"Pardon?"

"What, do you suppose, could have made him so wanton, that brother of mine?"

"I could not begin to imagine."

"No?"

"No. But I have taken enough of your day, sir. It is hardly my business, but I am happy to know your brother suffers no want of love."

I was standing so close to the enormous canvas that it trembled on its stretcher; a small ripple spread across the wall. I braced myself to say goodbye, but Francesco was unrelenting in his aggression.

"They never last long, these fancies of his. A single night, a few at the most, until the next one has caught his eye."

"It seems a life another man would envy, and yet it appears to inspire your reproach."

"I don't reproach my brother. His ways preserve him from heartache. He never waits for it to strike. He's learned his lesson."

I would hear no more and would not be detained any longer. Francesco followed, holding the drawing. He made to give it to me but settled for holding it up rather timidly.

"So you don't know her?"

I shook my head, where upon he ripped the portrait into pieces and threw them into the canal.

"By all that is sacred, I don't know anyone who looks like that."

The paper grew heavy. The ink ran.

6

SLOWLY EVERYTHING DISSOLVED. Outlines grew dim. The mist scattered the light, making everything seem less distinct. I caught an occasional glimpse of a gleaming naked body and heard sighs or gurgling water in the distance. Otherwise, I was able to feel alone. My thoughts relaxed. As the steam forced its way in, they fell apart like a sugarloaf in water. They didn't disappear but at last began to move, growing softer and smoother. They seemed lighter, if only because they were no longer knotted together. They drifted apart, as if the anxiety were dissipating over my whole body instead of bearing down on my stomach. Now and again a blast of hot breath burst through the mist, and Zélide loomed up. She was sitting opposite me, and every now and then she blew away the screen of white vapor that hung between us to let me know she was still there and make sure I was all right.

When I had returned to the Palazzo Cini after my excursion—agitated and reproaching myself for the wretched curiosity that had led me to discover more than I would have wished to know from Francesco—Zélide was standing in front of the house on the small bridge to the Campo San Vio. Unexpectedly, she removed my mask. One glance was enough. She understood without inquiring. Without knowing what had happened, she followed a natural impulse, like a mother comforting a child who has fallen, not by stroking the injury and wailing but softly, simply by making her child feel that she shares the pain. Brooking no objections, she packed me into a gondola and took me to the baths in Cannaregio. There she undressed me, bathed me, and wrapped me in a sheet, before leading me by the hand into the steam room. I shrank wordlessly into a corner on one of the stone benches, my arms wrapped around my knees.

"Shame is one of the basest of urges," said Zélide. "I place it at the bottom of the ladder of civilized feeling, between revenge and jealousy. It's a destructive force, fed by fear." I heard her close by but could not see her. "We carry this pernicious impulse within us as one of nature's burdens, but we must fight against it. We must!"

With that she appeared, her face suddenly close to mine.

"Why fear what *is*?" she whispered. I looked her in the eyes. To judge from my discomfort, I don't believe we had ever been so close. A few beads of water ran down her forehead, the last hanging from her nose. "Won't you resist this shame, Galatea? Please. It's not too late. I'll help you." She took my hand, squeezing it in encouragement. "If I can so easily see what *was,* why should you expect that others can't see as well?"

She moved away again, opening a trail through the clouds to lie down on the bench across from mine. Turning her back to me, she stretched and groaned contentedly.

"The joy of nakedness. I love it all the more in the company of others. Can you feel that? To defy the impulse to shame, to live above it."

Her voice was fading, and I imagined her dozing in the thickening mist. Then I heard the sound of her damp skin coming unstuck from the smooth stone as she turned over.

"Really, chastity is a scruple only for the lowest class. The unlettered and frightened need their rules and prohibitions to make sense of the world. Among their betters, the custom is quite unknown. I have yet to visit a court where it enjoyed any prestige."

I was persuaded not by her rhetoric but by an inner realization: I could do it, I decided. Indeed I should, for what hope did I have to be the object of such ardent desire again? I undid the sheet and laid it to one side. I blew hard a few times until she came into view, then let her calmly gaze upon what she had coveted for so long. We blew the hot air back and forth, and nothing more came between us.

ZÉLIDE WAS ALREADY SICK. But the poison was destroying her from inside, so that outwardly she remained the same until the end, and for a long time I suspected nothing. She kept her pain from me as long as she could, afraid perhaps that anticipating the inevitable I would seek another position. I stayed in her service four more years, all the while living in Vincennes.

THE FIRST MONTHS seemed a paradise. For days on end we wandered the streets of Paris together.

Zélide was nowhere more popular than in the most scintillating circles of Parisian society. We visited scores of scholars and magistrates who were anxious to hear of her journey and her discoveries near Naples. Wherever we went, I was never introduced as less than an equal, a cherished companion. As a consequence I was expected as never before to converse on all kinds of subjects, and I learned how one did so in the French style, the challenge like a juggler's, to keep the most improbable thoughts in the air for as long as possible. When the hemorrhaging began and Zélide took to bed, she refused any ministering except from me. The decline lasted more than three years. In the end I laid her out and buried her myself. There was a testament in which I was named. The bulk of her fortune had been consumed by her intellectual inquiries, "squandered," as the notary put it. The remainder passed by law to the children of her deceased husband. To me, she left all the metal and glass apparatus she had accumulated in her years of experimentation. The stable and the coach houses were full of this arcane paraphernalia, and it took me three months just to draw up an inventory. In the end I found a coppersmith willing to buy the lot for five louis d'or, just enough to sustain me for two months.

THE WEAKER SHE GREW, the more desperately Zélide had clung to "science," although it became less and less clear what this actually meant to her. Her insistent pursuit of vague and irrational interests only alienated her from her friends and acquaintances. She plunged into the wildest of enterprises, as if believing deep down that they offered some chance of a cure. As the fashion for science had by this time spread beyond imagining in Europe, and new disciplines were appearing like mushrooms following a rain shower, the distinction between serious scholarship and quackery grew more difficult to determine. Many frauds profited from Zélide's indiscriminate curiosity, and as hard facts betrayed her the succor of fantasy was rewarded.

Although I did my best to separate the wheat from the chaff and drove more than a few charlatans from the temple, the peace they brought Zélide soon outweighed any allegiance to truth. One of her obsessions was with horseless transport. To this end, she acquired from the Papin heirs the original plans for a steamship, which she intended to build on the Marne. To generate the requisite steam, the vessel would have needed to carry so much wood as to leave almost no room for the crew, let alone freight, but that was a small matter to her. She brought an engineer over from England to explain the workings of Newcomen's steam pump, a machine of gigantic pistons and cylinders devised half a century ago and abandoned as impractical. When neither Meyer's Dutch steam engine nor a pneumatic pump proved better suited, Zélide had the salon cleared to demonstrate a machine that produced static electricity with the help of what was called a Leyden jar. The terrifying spectacle attracted the better half of Paris.

Zélide continued to receive the curious until she concluded angrily that they were drawn less by the prospect of a potential boon to humanity than the spectacle in the salon. Frustrated by her inability to harness the natural force she could see with her own eyes and, even worse, unable to provide any reasonable proof or explanation for its very existence, she surrendered the last of her critical faculties. *Observo ergo est* became her creed: If she could see it, it was true. This cleared the way for a variety of confidence men equal to the task of providing plausible demonstrations. These included a young man from Neuchâtel who built androids, mechanical puppets that could write, compose music, and play chess; the "Count of Saint-Germain," who proved the effectiveness of his elixir of life by relating how he himself, as an acquaintance of Jesus, had witnessed His miracles in Canaan; and a doctor who promised to treat Zélide's illness by means of tyromancy, the practice of reading the future from a piece of cheese.

WHEREAS ONCE SHE had involved me in all her experiments, now she had retreated too far into her own world to share them with me. My skepticism disturbed her. Our conversations became colder, and in the end I helped her more as a servant than as a friend, a lackey who still proffered advice, however unbidden. In this way we both lived satisfactorily. In the last few weeks our conversations regained some of their old intimacy. By then she was bedridden, though no less absorbed by the drawing board she always kept within reach. She designed airships, sometimes three or four a day, each with a different shape and principle of levitation.

She had come up with this idea not long before, after we had seen a fish reach the surface of the pond in the courtyard by gulping air. It filled its body until it was quite round, then floated effortlessly. Once it had had enough of the surface, it let the air escape and sank to the bottom again. "If this principle works in water," Zélide said suddenly, "why not in air?" She became convinced of being in range of the discovery that would cause her to be remembered for centuries, if only she had enough time left to develop the concept. Anyone else would have approached the matter practically and rationally, by first formulating the laws that governed the principle, but Zélide, who could hear the ticking of the clock, skipped that step. After all, her emotions told her that she was on the right track. That was enough for her, and to avoid wasting any time she went straight to dreaming about the applications of her new invention. She produced big colorful sheets, scribbled full with springs, cogs, and puzzling formulae. Any technical principles that might have been present disappeared at crucial moments behind mind-boggling patterns or colorful balloons. The crews of the flying ships were imagined in detail: The aviators wore neat uniforms, and the passengers leaned over the railings.

If I dared vex her by asking how her machines could ever take flight, she reacted as if stung. "That's the secret!" she replied, disclosing only that they would be driven by what she called *soupe*. This liquid was activated by another, even more mysterious fluid. The latter, green in color, needed to be mixed with water before being dripped—an illustration depicted the process—onto hot coals to produce a pink gas that would lift the machines off the ground. I could only assume her disease was now devouring her brain. To look at, she was as beautiful as ever, but she was so feverish that I decided to torment her no longer with reality.

The moments of clarity, even as they grew briefer and less frequent, continued until the end, though often she would cry like a child suddenly finding he has lost his way. In those hours I sat close beside her as my mother would have done.

"What will you do?" she asked.

"I'll tell the cook to make some broth, and then we'll try to eat some of it together."

"Not now!" she snapped, ever more impatient with the quotidian. "Later. When I'm gone, what will you do then?"

"Have no fear," I said. "There will be no end of things to keep me busy!" My frivolous tone backfired, and for a moment it seemed she would sink into melancholy.

"Perhaps that's the worst of it," she mumbled softly to herself. "Everything goes on, and I shall never know how it ends."

"Don't worry about me. The whole world is before me. What shall happen I'll find out in due course."

Zélide tried to sit up straight. As I straightened her pillows she grabbed me urgently by the wrist.

"A person can weigh up infinite possibilities, but there is always one he most desires. Remember that!"

I promised that I would, but my tone annoyed her. Now she heard condescension in the kindly voice I had used often these last few days to soothe her and avoid awkwardness. She would not be placated and briefly recovered her old passion.

"Reason offers us many possibilities at once. Intuition infallibly chooses the best. Remember this and you cannot err; you
will always make the right choice."

"Always?"

"Always!"

"Even in affairs of the heart?"

"Most of all. It's so simple, and yet so many spend a whole
life without seeing it. Listen: It's a question of closing your eyes
and doing the first thing that comes to mind. Do you hear me?
That's all there is to it. One is only ever capable of wanting one
thing at a time."

We sat hand in hand for a long while. She would live on for
days afterward, but this wordless moment was our letting go of
each other; we both knew it. I gave her another kiss and went to
fetch the broth, but when I returned she had already picked up
her drawing board and returned to her airships. With her
tongue sticking out between her teeth, she sketched a married
couple, passengers, drinking tea amid the clouds at a table on
deck. Zélide wrote beside it that the table should be set with
damask and genuine silver.

THAT WHOLE YEAR had been unusually warm. In August the
heat became unbearable. The days were scorching and the
nights brought almost no relief. Leaving Vincennes I took just a
few books and the clothes I could wear, but even before reaching the highway I was forced to shed the light coat and abandon
it under a bush.

I was twenty years old, without family, friends, or possessions apart from the lessons Zélide and Monsieur de Pompignac
had taught me. For all her abiding exultations, she had found no
more peace in death than he had in professing the faith of rea-

son. I felt myself free to discover my own way. Years before, on leaving Pasiano, I had headed south. This time I chose the opposite direction.

Amsterdam was one of the first great cities to which Monsieur de Pompignac had awakened me. I'd seen it in engravings many times in the books he gave me to read, the most important of which had all been printed in Holland, where, he told me, both Descartes and Spinoza had found refuge. Hollanders, he said, were clean and tolerant, prosperous and Christian; they believed in the equality of all people and in free expression. Traders the world over, they imported not just pepper and coffee but also the beliefs of other nations. Locke and Bayle had thrived there and praised the city. From Signora Morandi's library in Bologna, I knew the *Systema Naturæ* and the *Genera Plantarum* with all the flowers and spicae that Linnaeus had studied in Amsterdam's Botanical Gardens. I had only to think of the city's name to see before me a paradise where, amid all the flowers of the world, the human mind flourished and all the branches of science grew freely.

THE TREES along the road from Vincennes to Paris had been pruned in the style then favored by Louis XV. They provided hardly any shade, and even the birds struggled to survive beneath them. I searched in vain for a carriage that could take me to the Marais, where coaches left for the north. Even before I had covered the first of the six miles to town, I was drenched with sweat. When I came to the bridge I did not hesitate to refresh myself in the cool water in the stream beneath its dark arches. Then I put on as few clothes as I could to remain respectable, fashioning my petticoat into a pouch in which to carry some of the rest. When I climbed back up to the road, I saw a man approaching, immersed in whatever he was reading.

He didn't look up or around and had come within ten steps of me when he suddenly froze. He shrieked and reached for his head as if he had been struck by a rock. But the blow could only have been the words he had just read. He gasped like a wounded man and flailed around looking for something to hold on to. I ran to help him to the ground. When I spoke, he did not respond. Taking him to have been affected by the strong sun, I hurried off to fetch some water, but when I returned he was too elated to drink.

"It's true, though, isn't it?" he shouted, grabbing both my hands as though drawing a lady into a dance. "Why is everybody always so curious to know how things fit together? They only calculate out of greed, and without injustice there would be no need to study law! Imagine: without wars and conspiracies, no history to tell!"

From this raving I understood his affliction to be far worse than a touch of the sun, and I tried to disentangle myself. When the man saw me frightened, he apologized as best he could.

"Please excuse me. I was going to Vincennes. A friend is imprisoned there," he blurted. "I'm on my way to visit him, and I have just read . . . I could have taken any book, but in the morning I chose this, by chance. Incredible!" His words failing him, he pressed the *Mercure de France* into my hands and pointed out an advertisement. I seized the opportunity to escape and left him by the side of the road, still dazed.

Only later, when I had secured a seat on a coach heading north at a trot, did I read the advertisement. It was an announcement by the Academy of Dijon of an essay competition. The theme to be expounded: *Whether the progress of science and the arts contributed to the deterioration or to the improvement of individual morals.* I had no immediate opinion except to observe that it hadn't made the streets any safer. Glad of having escaped the madman unscathed, I mumbled a prayer. I threw the paper out the window of the coach, but until Senlis at least I felt a vague melancholy. It was not unlike what I had felt one night when as a little girl at Pasiano I sat playing on the floor of the countess's room. Hearing the adults outside on the terrace, I could tell they were speaking with passion of something greater than all our lives, and content though I was at play, I struggled to make out what was being said, realizing at last that I couldn't. At that moment I felt a gloom I hadn't known before.

III

Theatrum Amatorium

*E*very autumn my parents left me to spend a week or two at my uncle's farm in Belluno. Boar were more common there than in Pasiano, and the deer seemed less wary. What's more, my parents explained, the partridges gathered in the open fields and flew head-on at the hunters. While my father was off hunting with his brother, my mother and her sister-in-law would look for blackberries, red currants, and mushrooms; at midday, everyone came together to butcher and salt the game, clean and dry the mushrooms, and cook and preserve the fruit.

The pleasure of my parents' return always erased the loneliness I felt while they were away. They unpacked their heavily laden bags in the kitchen, arranged the delicacies we would be eating until spring, and let me taste the candied walnuts and red currant jelly. Until I grew too old to believe them, my mother would tell me stories about my uncle and aunt's house, how they lived on a candy mountain in the Land of Cockaigne, next to a lake of wine.

The autumn after I turned six, my parents decided that I was old enough to go with them. The mountain turned out to be hidden under a thick forest, and the lake beside the small farm was covered with a black layer of rotting leaves. My uncle and aunt were simple folk. They had one son, Geppo, whom *they loved almost to excess. He was about ten years older than I but slow-witted. And so from the time he could walk they kept him tied in the barnyard as they went about their chores. When in the morning we headed off into the forest, we heard behind us my cousin bellowing pitifully and straining at his tether. My aunt was always desperate to run back and comfort him, but she had learned that the effort changed nothing. At midday the boy sat by the big table. As we set to work, it seemed our activity entertained him, and he remembered nothing of his earlier abandonment. Sometimes he helped to sort the nuts.*

On warm days they let him swim. Swimming was his passion. He could race through the water for hours without rest. Broadly built and powerful, he seemed inexhaustible in his element. Still, they never let him go without a strong rope tied around his waist. My uncle held the other end at all times, and when he felt an unexpected tug because his son had dived too deeply or swum too far from shore, he would rush to the boy's rescue, even though my cousin was by far the better swimmer.

The first two years I hardly dared to approach Geppo alone, but in the autumn that followed I got to know him better. I had twisted my ankle on a rocky path and so was obliged to stay behind when the others went into the woods. One morning, out of boredom, I hopped into the yard to look at my feebleminded cousin. He beckoned me and tried to grab my leg. When I let him take it, he turned out to have a gentle touch. For at least an hour, he massaged my foot and my swollen ankle, devoting himself completely to the task as if there were nothing else to be done in the world, and by the time he had finished I could stand without pain.

After that we became good friends. I told him about Pasiano and our lives there, the countess and her grand visitors. One day I was startled when Geppo interrupted my account. It was the first time I had heard him speak, and though he ended most sentences laughing uncontrollably I could understand him well enough.

We played together all the following week, and I swam with him until I tired. At some moment I sighed in the cruel way of children about how terrible it must be to have your parents tie you up like a goat. As usual, he didn't react, and it was only after I had been prattling about other things an hour later that he stopped me in mid-sentence.

"Yes," Geppo exclaimed, loud and clear. "They love me because my head is poor." At this he laughed so hard he started coughing. When he had recovered, he added, "That shows them how rich their heads are."

When we arrived in Belluno the next year, my uncle and my cousin were dead. They had drowned one day in summer when Geppo's rope got snagged on a branch while he was diving to the bottom of the lake. It trapped the boy, and then my uncle— trying too long to rescue him—became ensnared as well. That autumn my father went hunting alone, while my mother and I stayed with my aunt. She was remarkably stoic. My mother cooked the red currants, I sugared them, and my aunt mashed them through an iron sieve. Her sorrow was silent, but suddenly I saw big round tears falling into the pulp.

"I was given so much," she said, to no one in particular. "Surely it would have been a sin not to seize that happiness with both hands?" Awaking from her reverie, she saw me sitting beside her and embraced me as if holding on for her life, and I was left with mashed fruit in my hair. It was all she would ever show me of her grief, but that winter, when we went to draw on our supply of red currant jelly, all the pots tasted salty.

I

THE WOMEN SIT on low chairs, trying to keep their backs to the onlookers. They hold their heads down and their shoulders up, for fear of being struck by something hard. They would do better to turn around, at least to see the imminent assault and thereby perhaps to evade it, but the glares of the patrons are more hurtful than the rubbish they throw. Officially, throwing things at the prisoners is no longer permitted, but such sport is traditional; for a small charge above the price of admission, the doorkeeper allows one to enter with a few harmless odds and ends. Some conceal green apples or worse among the balls of paper and the vegetable rinds; they want value for money and feel cheated without the pleasure of making a whore yelp. Anyone who succeeds in drawing a bit of blood instantly becomes a hero to the crowd. There is even a bit of wagering as to who will prevail in this way, although the women, who never look up, are always last to know.

The Amsterdam spin house is no different from the ones in Delft, Leiden, and The Hague. For travelers to Holland, visiting at least one is de rigueur and a most economical diversion; for just two stivers, visitors can stay as long as they like. There are always a few overgrown lads hoping to impress their fiancées by abusing the captives; it surprised me at first to see some perfectly respectable ladies excited by such spectacle. The prison is also recommended in all the travel journals, so that no foreigner leaves Amsterdam without experiencing this uniquely Dutch attraction.

"Imagine! You live right around the corner and have never come before!" exclaimed Mr. Jamieson. He spoke without taking his eyes off the women on show, so he failed to notice my unease. "Where else could you find such theater?"

He then asked me which measures they used to force the women to reform and how one could tell which prisoners were thieves and which were whores, as they were all equally ugly in his eyes.

My American friend thought he was amusing me. In the last few months, we had often been out and about together in Amsterdam, and until now our amusements had been of the most lighthearted kind. Jamieson is a gentle man at heart and not immune to the simple pleasures of life. For years he did his own hunting, skinning, and tanning, work that left him with rough manners and hands like pumice. But he has become famous for his furs and suedes, which are worn at all the courts of Europe, thanks to a secret technique that allows him to smooth out every irregularity, down to the smallest capillaries. Having held a monopoly over bear and beaver in the valleys of the Hudson for several years, he arrived in Holland in late summer with the aim of furthering his European custom.

We meet, as I mentioned, every Thursday. He arrives in the afternoon, and a long stroll typically precedes dinner. Sometimes he takes me to a dance hall as well, less often to a soirée where the favor of his company has been requested. It was never a set plan to meet with such regularity; we simply fell into the habit. And on that evening when fate would play its nasty trick on me, he was kept off his feet by a touch of the gout, and I had moped a bit during the day and felt myself at loose ends.

Though I was quick to remind myself that Jamieson is twenty years my senior, unattractive, and hardly a prospect for marriage, I had come to depend on his attentions and the pleasant times he arranged with such ardor.

I HAD NO REASON at all to suppose that this evening's surprise would be different. He collected me at home in the usual way. We wouldn't go far, walking out onto the Oudezijds Achterburgwal. When he stopped just a few doors away and stood beaming with anticipation before the grand facade of the spin house, I saw my chance to protest slip away.

In the attic, where the whores and other women in need of correction are exhibited in a large cage, I took the opportunity to explain to Mr. Jamieson that my want of acquaintance with the spectacle so near my dwelling was not a matter of ignorance—quite the contrary. I delivered my little lecture on the institution in a most dispassionate voice, trying to avoid provoking those incredulous sympathetic gasps that to my annoyance would sometimes escape this skinner of animals when he heard tell of life's rougher side. Nor had I any wish to embarrass these poor women further.

When I had finished, we fell as silent as the women themselves, who never speak in the presence of onlookers. Their punishment nowadays is no longer to spin but rather to sew, linen in particular. Most have bandaged fingers, because the thread so abrades their flesh as to expose and sometimes even cut through tendons. For a while all we heard was the sound of working hands, fabric drawn through fingertips and occasionally the whipping sound of a sheet being folded with sudden fierce gestures.

This wasn't enough for the other spectators. One of them whooped that if the whores were not even to speak, he wanted his two stivers back. Another egged him on by shouting that in the alleys off the Kalverstraat they'd lend you "a helping hand" for the same price. At this, the couple who watched over the fallen women's work and earnings, the house father and mother, so to speak, interceded, poking their charges with sticks to encourage a bit less modesty. Most submitted, turning reluctantly to face us, only to meet with even more abuse. The visitors blasted the ugliness of the women, adding that any customer of theirs surely must be blind, or perhaps a leper.

Under the rain of prods and curses, one woman still refused to show herself. I stared at her back to avoid the gaze of the others in the cage. She shivered. Her fingers curled tightly around the arms of her chair, as if she was at pains to maintain her defiance. The crowd hungrily took up the challenge she presented. Now their most obscene curses were directed at her alone in the hope of breaking her.

This display was unbearable. I took Mr. Jamieson by the arm. With his face full of shame, he apologized in his childish manner, and we tried to make our way out, but, having smelled blood, the crowd had no intention of parting to let us through. One man struck the back of Jamieson's head, and I was forced up against the palisade that separated the prisoners from the visitors. In that instant the solitary unyielding woman was also struck in the back, by a piece of wood someone had smuggled in. She caught her breath and rose from her chair as the whooping subsided into an expectant silence. Everyone was cowed except one lout who hurled a gob of spit at her in an attempt to provoke her further. Without wiping his spittle from her neck, she paused indifferently.

I seized the chance to squeeze between the spectators and make for the door. Just then the woman in the cage lurched forward, like a wild animal. She threw herself against the bars with all her might, so the whole the attic hummed and the visitors recoiled in shock. I did too, but I was now nearest the cage, and before I knew it she had reached through the bars and grabbed me by the arm, pulling me toward her as if to take a hostage from among her tormentors. Only my veil separated me from the awful stench issuing from her rotten mouth. When I was able to look, I saw a nose eaten away by syphilis, a face as drawn and ravaged as if the devil himself had danced upon it in hobnailed boots. Without a dose of mercury she would soon be dead.

A sudden sympathy mixed with my horror. "Oh, God," I mumbled, "you poor soul, I am so sorry."

Unexpectedly the grip weakened. Her face relaxed. Wide-eyed, she tried to peer through my veil, perhaps imagining she knew me. When I attempted to break free of her grasp, her fury was renewed, her claws now deeper in my flesh and pulling me closer still. Like a miller caught in the cogs, I was pulled helpless toward her festering body. In my terror I screamed for help in my mother tongue and called out the first name that came to mind. I had not spoken it aloud since I was a girl. Now, without knowing why, I repeated it over and over.

When did I see my Giacomo in that silken Frenchman? In retrospect I can scarcely believe my recognition was not immediate, the very moment he was brought to my box at the theater, perhaps even when I heard his voice as the boatman paused under the bridge. In any case, when his wig blew off in the storm by the Amstel, there was no doubt. But even after the truth was plain, like St. Thomas I could not yet take it into my heart.

Of course, in my mind he had remained as when I last saw him: wide dark eyes set in an olive-hued face, cheeks downed with a faint boyish beard. Now the pallid face of middle-aged weariness admitted none of the easy laughter that had once entranced me, and the eyes, once full of liquid warmth, were those of a bird of prey, following some hapless creature. Perhaps never to have imagined Giacomo changed was the solace I had afforded myself when I disappeared from Pasiano. If we were not to change together, I could at least press into my memory the unexpected buds of the life we were to have shared.

But physiognomy alone could not explain my reluctance to see in the Frenchman the young man I had loved. Were only his outward aspect transformed, reason would have delivered me to comprehension. But his inner nature was even more altered, and of this too I had unknowingly enshrined a memory that did not admit of change. Beyond whatever mask experience had fashioned, the Giacomo I had kept in my heart these many years was known to me as one whose love for me was greater and better than mine for him. I had felt it always and had taken it for a sign that he knew more deeply than I what it was to love. Those who have felt the sweet bliss of this certitude will not doubt that it felt to me as firm as the ground beneath my feet. This nameless and indescribable knowledge was like that of an expectant mother who, feeling the life in her womb, never for a moment doubts that she will love the child or that the child will love her. An emotion like this doesn't reside in consciousness. We become aware of it only when we are so unfortunate as to be disabused of it. The loss fixes the mind on what we possessed, the disappointment on the defeat of innocent expectation. Thought gives it form and allows us to recognize it. Painfully and with gratuitous cruelty, reason exposes the betrayal of emotion.

THAT IS WHAT happened on the evening I described, when I witnessed the adult Giacomo kill his younger self as we bade each other good night under a light rain.

"She was a woman," he said—his only form of account for not finding his beloved waiting when he returned to Pasiano one spring. "She was a woman."

I closed the door without replying and listened mournfully as the sound of his footsteps receded down the Rusland.

FOR DAYS AFTERWARD my distraction was overwhelming. At night I paced the room. All day long, I lay restless in bed. Dressing, washing, and feeding myself—all the rituals of living—were neglected. I kept the shutters closed.

"*Ma, signora, avanti!*" ventured Danaë, when she came by with Giovanna after work to pay what was due me. She did her best to raise my spirits. "You really must come dancing with us tomorrow. The city is too sad without you! Just look at yourself; you look a fright. What's got into you?"

I felt humiliated: more ashamed than sorrowful. How could I, who had been so hardened by the struggle to survive, have let myself be undone by a perfectly predictable matter of fact? The years that made me unrecognizable had done likewise to my love. Perhaps, quite simply, with so much adversity to face every day, the thought had never occurred to me. It's just not possible to contemplate life while struggling to live it. Reflection is a luxury of those without worry for the future.

My happy memories were spare and still, like a scene on a canvas. But what painter stops to think about the curtains being taken down after the sitting, the blinds drawn, and the models returned home? What admirer of art would care to be reminded that, a moment later, the figures walk away from the window or rise from the couch, to speak coarsely, stretch, and relieve their bladders, anxious to strip off their gorgeous borrowed clothes and go to an alehouse? No one questions it: One wants the Last Supper, not the handmaid who clears the table, neither the crumbs nor the stains on the tablecloth nor the cat that licks the plates clean.

Giacomo lived on after our parting. And thank God. It was my most devout wish that he would forget me and that his life would be his own, unencumbered by what had become of mine. That living should have changed him was natural. But the bitterness born of his first betrayal, the contempt it had engendered for all other women, and the self-reproach that had made of our shared past the stuff of a lesson for every man to learn in his time—these were the unbearable fruits of some darkened fairy tale.

I tried to take comfort in his not having recognized me as he made his harsh report. But the comforting thought became a painful one: that he had spoken so freely, as he might have done with friends in Venice or strangers met at inns on the road, revealed that in his heart he accounted as some sort of cheap swindle what was my life's great tragedy. I could hear the biting bluster with which he regaled men with his story and gave his mistresses to know that he would not be fooled by their female tricks.

Would the tender Giacomo of Pasiano have ever changed into the cynical Jacques de Seingalt if I had listened to my girlish heart and not subdued my fierce desire with clear-eyed foresight? What if I had dared to show him myself ravaged, trusting to our love, letting life and nature run their course instead of sacrificing myself like some inane operatic heroine? In that case, I alone would have been disfigured; now we both were.

I WALLOWED three days in these lamentations, endlessly rehearsing the most painful sentences in our conversation on the Amstel, his professions of having fallen perpetual victim of feminine intrigue. And worst of all: that no one had ever truly loved him. It was not until the fourth day of my self-confinement that I suddenly remembered another thing he'd said, and with that I was finally propelled into action.

Having washed and dressed, I ventured out. At Izaak Duym's, south of the town hall, I bought a half ream of the finest writing paper and had it trimmed. At home I laid the sheets out; they remained unmarked until evening, when, hovering over them, I finally found these words:

Your Lordship,
My dear Chevalier,
    When we last met you proposed a double challenge:
    First, that I receive your courtship in order that I might discover you to be that rare exception, a man of feeling above his own satisfactions—a highly improbable condition, by my estimation.
    Second, that I present a woman whose love for you has left her the worse for it—a condition you call impossible.
    I am prepared to accept your wager, for want of other diversion and having by benefit of reason deduced that I cannot fail to emerge the winner. For if, my dear chevalier, you should prove an unexceptional man, the wager shall be mine. But if your professions be true, I shall win a few happy hours in your company. If we would then part as friends, as you predict, I shall have lost nothing, but should I find myself to be that unexampled thing, a woman wronged by you, my sorrow will be fast relieved when you pay me what I have won.
    If these conditions, which hold no promise of advantage for you, are understood, it shall please me to give you the benefit of my love.

Yours,
Galathée de Pompignac

The next day, which was Thursday, I received an invitation from Seingalt to accompany him to the theater to see *Harlequin Hulla* and sup with him afterward. I was somewhat piqued by this, as the comedy in question was staged on Saturdays only, and I am unaccustomed to being made to wait. Still, I was determined not to be brought low, since Thursday was Jamieson's regular day, and he was deserving of my full and cheerful attention. But I would have been less concerned about my American friend had I known that this was the day he would surprise me with an excursion to the spin house.

As THE WHORE dug her talons into my flesh, Jamieson tried to pull me loose, but in her madness she was stronger. The house father rushed up to answer my cries for help and entered the cage. He seized the harpy by the shoulders, but, unable to subdue her thus, he put a stick across her throat, pulling back on it with all his might to choke her into submission. Her grip didn't relax until she had almost no breath at all, but even in surrender she had enough life left in her to claw at me a final time. She managed to rip away a strip of my smock and catch the hem of my veil, the removal of which produced a general merriment. The whore collapsed, gasping. But from the floor, her wild-eyed stare was more intense than ever, as she studied my face through the bars while plucking at the selvage of my veil.

Mr. Jamieson had never seen my scars. For a moment he inclined his head slightly toward me, as if not quite sure what he was seeing.

"Ah," he said, without disgust or pity but rather something akin to relief, as if he had found something he had long been searching for. Then, very briefly, he laid his hand on my cheek. I shivered at the cool of his touch. In all these years, no one had touched me there. Then, without a word, he laid his scarf around my shoulders and I wound my shame in it. Putting an arm around me, he led me to the exit.

"Go on, run!" the fury yelled at my back. "Run as far as you like. The truth'll catch up to you still. Did you come for some fun, you filthy Jew's whore? To see it from the other side for once? Come to have a good laugh, did you? Now you've been recognized. The laughter is for you!"

2

THE DUTCH compare whores to horses. The bargeman's nags, in the local parlance, are the lowly streetwalkers. The cart horses are the ones displayed in windows and the gaming-house molls. The harness horse is the term for room cats and the tarts of the more discreet brothels, who feel themselves superior to the rest. And the saddle horses are those women who let themselves be kept, almost honorably, like wives.

Over the years I've seen the inside of every sort of stable. I had no choice. There is no type of yoke I have not stooped to take up. It's the simple truth.

WHEN I FIRST arrived in Amsterdam from Paris, I still went about unveiled. The water everywhere in the city was black and smooth, and my reflection followed me over every bridge and along every canal. But when people looked at me on the street, they invariably saw my disfigurement first. I could almost feel their eyes glide down the side of my face and throat. There would be a momentary loss of composure, as their minds decided whether their reaction was to be mainly horror or pity. The former always pained me less.

People had been approaching me that way for years. I could

hardly remember another way, and I had long since ceased to be conscious of any hurt. But in Holland it was different. It is a small country whose people are crowded together. The Dutch are at pains not to be lost in the multitude, and each one typically strives to distinguish himself from his neighbors. In this land of individualism, differences are not politely smoothed over but are emphasized, especially for foreigners and newcomers. Indeed, the peculiarities of others can be tremendously helpful in moderating the belief in one's own perfection. And difference turns out to be fairly tolerable as long as it is made perfectly clear. In this sense, my scars were a godsend, a gift of fellowship. Strangers and near strangers remarked upon them openly, not just to each other but to me as well. Those I had only just met inquired solicitously about the cause of my disfigurement and the sorrow it must have caused me, as if a certain practiced empathy were good manners. I took their inquisitiveness to be of a piece with the famed tolerance of this land that had attracted the great freethinkers, but I confess it did make me uneasy.

It was some time before I realized a thing assumed among the Dutch: Tolerance is not the equal of acceptance. Indeed, the two are more nearly opposites, the former sometimes serving as a subtle means of repression. To accept another is to embrace him unconditionally, now and always. But to tolerate him is to suggest in the same breath that he is rather an inconvenience, like a nagging pain or an unpleasant odor demanding temporary forbearance. In this way tolerance serves at the pleasure of the mood. And there are other limitations. Once properly perceived, every beneficiary of tolerance is obliged to remain as first identified and labeled, like some poison in an apothecary's cabinet. The potential for terror is in the fantasy of the alchemist's transmutation, whereby one thing becomes another. And so you have the deeper truth of the country's vaunted individualism: It maintains the order of things. No earthly good is served for a saddle horse to be mistaken for a nag.

THERE WAS ANOTHER consequence of so much freedom: People led very private lives. It's a simple fact that people feel more fellowship when groaning under a strict regime. Amsterdammers are by nature reserved. Those I chatted with on my daily walks never invited me to their homes. Everywhere else in Europe I had found it easy to live from hand to mouth, but here preserving the union of body and soul was a labor. The city's great prosperity was over. There were many more hands than jobs. I had hoped to pay my way as a tutor of French but was unable to find a situation with any of the wealthy families, despite more often than not speaking better French than the master of the house himself. The fact of my having grown up on a country estate and learned everything about running a large household at my mother's knee was also a matter of indifference in Amsterdam's relatively small canal houses. I tried in vain to obtain work as a lady's companion or even a lady's maid in a respectable home. Initially I put the rejections down to my appearance, but even the hint of such a thought filled those of whom I besought a situation with fervid indignation; such sentiments, I was assured, were quite foreign to the people of this country. To judge by their chagrin, one would have thought that, on the contrary, my appearance was of some advantage, and so more was the shame that the position had always just been filled.

I was forced in time to give up my comfortable guesthouse and lodge with a widow on the Oude Waal who rented out a back room with a bed. I tried in vain to secure a place in a shop. One merchant referred me to a workhouse that produced cheap imitations of Ghent lace; I spent a day and a half there before it was decided that my tendency to prick my fingers and bleed on the wares disqualified me. At Pasiano, it turned out, I had learned precious few of the skills expected of a young woman. In one of the coach houses in the Kerkstraat, I found three days' work as a groom before the owner decided that it was an unseemly labor for a woman. But I had enjoyed working with my hands, and so, calling on what I had learned watching my father, I made some inquiries among the estates in the area about prospects for service among the foresters or the hunters. All for naught: There was hardly any timber or game to be found in the environs of the city, which for miles around was nothing but water and marsh.

My first experiences of candor were rather refreshing. When I would offer myself at some inn as a maid or waitress, I was told forthrightly that my appearance would deter custom, either by ruining the appetite of patrons or by discouraging them even from entering. Finally, at a fish market, I found someone willing to add my name to the roll of those waiting for the first return of a large fleet to port, when women would be needed to gut the catch. The nets alas returned empty, and life remained expensive. I sold Count Antonio's *Dom Bougre* for much less than it was worth. Within six weeks I had exhausted the proceeds and was on my way to a pawnshop. There I left the pendant my grandfather had made, the mirror with the eyes of the saint. I received in return a pittance and a miserably short term in which I could redeem my property. Before surrendering it to the indifferent pawnbroker, I kissed the dear memento a last time and swore I would not lose it.

On my way out of the shop a stranger accosted me. This was unusual in Dutch cities and I was immediately on my guard, but he was a respectable-looking gentleman. He expressed a familiar interest in my scars but, as I would discover, he was a surgeon and his interest professional. His wish was to present me to his students as an exemplary victim of smallpox; he offered to pay me for my trouble.

THE CLASSROOM WAS dark and unwelcoming when I entered. There was a pungent smell of alcohol and camphor. I removed my outer garments in the adjoining room, among the shadows of some frightening inanimate presences—skeletons and stuffed animal carcasses—but the prospect of a bit of money was enough to pluck up my courage. It was only when they opened the uppermost shutters of this former weigh-house that I discovered myself standing in the middle of an amphitheater. Sitting around me were some twenty young men. They were, I had been assured, apprentice surgeons, guild members, and so only professionally interested in the human body.

The professor spoke in a soft, friendly voice and did nothing without first asking my permission. After describing things in Latin, he summarized his observations in French, apparently for my benefit, though all were astonished that I could follow even in the vernacular what was said. In essence they were studying the distortion of the skin and the difference between eroded tissues and those where the original pock had healed without bursting. Examining my throat and shoulders, the professor pointed out places where the pustule had erupted *subcutaneously,* spreading poison under the skin. He asked me to move a certain way, and when I remarked that I had always found that particular motion difficult, he explained that this was owing to the presence of hard scar tissue in the muscles, a peculiar vestige of the pox, which he promised to expose on the dissecting table later that day. I made a sign of the cross for the poor soul who would take my place for that demonstration, but nowhere that I looked—among the skeletons, detached limbs, and stillbirths in bottles—was any comfort for the spirit to be found.

The lecture lasted an hour. I had been paid as promised and was dressing in the adjoining room when the professor came in. Given the experience of the past hour, it may seem odd that I grabbed my skirt to cover my nakedness. He seemed amused by this modesty and said he had brought a tincture which he believed might reduce the tension of my scars and make the horny skin more supple. He tipped some of the liquid into the palm of his hand and mixed it with oil.

I could flatter myself to report I was confused and hesitant, but I don't believe it was so. I voiced no unease when he rubbed the oil into my skin. When his hands wandered, I made no attempt to stop them. He took me standing. As grateful as a child, he pushed up against me. When a satisfied bubble of spit emerged at the corner of his grinning lips, the ruddy face of the Count of Montereale, that sinister man made innocent in his pleasure, appeared in my mind. As we danced our solitary dance, a lioness, a swan, a crocodile, and a snake looked on, along with the mounted skin of an anatomized criminal and— the room's showpiece—the skeleton of an elephant, its ribs swaying along with us.

This was the start of my new life in Amsterdam. I left the anatomical theater feeling myself liberated and without regret. An hour later, after retrieving my grandfather's pendant from the pawnbroker, I still had money enough to live for a week. I stopped wearing my precious mirror and buried it among my other possessions. I could not continue on this course in the sight of Lucia's eyes.

SOMETIMES, WHEN the full weight of reality was bearing down on me, I wept bitterly. At those times I was fully aware of the treasure I had surrendered. I knew I had made this irrevocable, perhaps inevitable, choice of my own free will, but its sorrow haunted my nights all the same. In dreams my parents appeared before me so vividly I would awake to find my hands outstretched as if to touch them. Sometimes I spoke to them out loud. I begged their forgiveness. I comforted them too, telling them not to worry, despite never having heard from me. As I woke, I would remember how far away they were, assuming they were both still alive. Otherwise I was at peace within myself, believing in my heart that the work was outside me; while changing my social position it could not touch the essence of my being.

THERE WAS A SAILOR, a merchant seaman. As soon as his ship docked, he would come to me for a taste of life. One day he recalled how, in rough weather off the coast of Guinea, he had been knocked off the storm jib and into the water. He thrashed, of course, like a man possessed. Terrified, he screamed for help, but no one heard him, only the sharks. He saw their fins circling, but as soon as they found him and were drawing closer, his fear disappeared. The thought that he was completely lost and at the end of his journey filled him from one moment to the next with a profound peace, a satisfaction he had never before known. He stopped fighting and gave himself over to the waves, as a man might to a woman's bosom, he said. He was in this bliss when a boat appeared, disturbing everything. His shipmates beat back the sharks. When they threw the drowning man a line, he seemed almost indifferent. He had passed a point and no longer wanted to return. Assuming he had lost his senses, they struggled to drag him into the boat.

I have known that kind of peace, a grace to be found only in the deepest hopelessness. To those unacquainted with it, it is an incomprehensible mystery. As long as life presents the possibility of escape, our minds calculate at full speed. We feel our fate is in our hands and seek the best outcome, though we are terrified of making the wrong decision. But it is this sense of free will, not the prospect of even the worst outcome, that brings us to despair. Where there is the least room for doubt, there can be no rest. Only with the assurance that our fate is sealed can we stop thinking and dare trust at last to our intuition. Without hesitation, surrendering to our first impulse, we find peace. And in so doing, we survive.

That at least is how I came through the deepest humiliations. Shame was embedded in my flesh like a harpoon. Untouched, it caused me no pain, but whenever I tried to pull it out the wound was deepened. Over the last few years, I have made many decisions with this knowledge in the back of my mind. After all, it wasn't the first time I had been forced to accept my life's branching off from the route I had plotted in my dreams.

I learned from my merchant seaman in that sense as well. Once he had hoped to become a captain and set his own course, but in time it was clear that his hope would be disappointed. By then his work was heavy. It broke his back and cut his hands. It made him ill and dirty and homesick. But though he had saved a tidy sum, after each voyage he signed up again. It was, he discovered, the journey itself that he most enjoyed.

I RETURNED to the anatomical theater several times, but the professor's ardor had faded. On my final visits, for the usual fee, I was persuaded to stand beside the dissecting table for a practical demonstration. If Signora Morandi can bear it, I thought, so can I. During the lecture I would give evidence of the function of some muscle in the living body, whereupon the professor would cut the same tissue out of the cadaver on the table and hold it up for his students. Once he pressed the dead specimen against my bare back to show how short a particular muscle was at rest and how far it could stretch from its point of attachment. I didn't flinch, but it was then I resolved not to return.

After this I worked with great industry to support myself in my little room but soon aroused the suspicions of the widow with whom I was lodging. She had banned relations with men under her roof and threw me out, despite my arrears. My decline was rapid. I went from a bed to straw, and from straw to a bare floor.

I DO NOT RELATE all this calamity under the illusion that it reveals anything about me in particular. Better women have gone down this same path, as have ones who were worse. The story serves only to evoke the times and the conditions in which I resolved to survive. They were hard years. Holland's dominion over the seas had passed to England. In Amsterdam there were thousands of women like me.

As a streetwalker, I never frequented the Kalverstraat, where the twopenny whores plied their trade. Late in the afternoon, I would walk past the carpenters' yards to a park known as the Plantage and promenade there at my leisure. I solicited patrons with a glance, and the transaction occurred between bushes or, in winter, in the shelter of the orangery. It was customary to remain silent. This was crucial, actually. It allowed some kind of illusion to be maintained, in which a man could fantasize as he wished. One might have gone to one of the inns, but they had a bad name. Most men were afraid to be seen in one, and I myself preferred the outdoors. Even when the business was unpleasant, I found a certain consolation in the surroundings—whether in the green foliage around my head or the sharp twigs scratching my skin. The rustling of branches moving in time with us. The elastic pressure of a sapling trunk against my back. Bark under my fingers. The warm, heady smells of moss, wood, and resin rising on a summer's evening as the cool night air drew the last of the dew up out of the ground. There were so many things to distract me from what was really happening. More than anything else, I remember my feet sinking slowly under the weight, deeper and deeper into the soil.

It's tempting to say that the Plantage took me back to my happiest years at Pasiano, where I was surrounded by nature, choosing my playmates from among the animals and riding the horses as they roamed the fields. I was unafraid and unjudged as a child, and nothing limited my happiness; no dangers overhung it. But that couldn't be said of the Amsterdam Plantage, where in my brief time as a streetwalker three bodies were discovered amid the brush, women like me whose labors had been compensated by a knife across the throat. Still, the verdure of the setting somehow made the most vile acts seem more natural. Later, in gaming houses or back rooms, there would be no escape from the bleakness. But here among the nettles, with the scent of roses in the air, my situation was so strange as to seem unreal. I took part without self-awareness. The only similarity with Pasiano: I remember no limits.

SOON ENOUGH, HOWEVER, I was press-ganged by a bully, one of the disreputable characters of the district who extort money for protection, mainly from the menace they themselves pose. He found a place for me at a whorehouse in the shadow of the Herring Packers' Tower, close to the port. It drew the dregs from among the dregs, being frequented mainly by the crews of East Indiamen. Every day ships moored, spilling out seamen who had not seen a woman in months. They inundated the city with money in their pockets, mad with lust. If we whores had not been there to meet this horde of savages and to give them some release, they might have raped all the city's daughters and mothers.

The work was hard and filthy. Most of them were unwashed and unshaven. Even worse: They had imagined the most bizarre fantasies in the long months at sea, grotesque fancies that had preyed on their lonely minds. Often I ended up in a tangle of bodies like some criminal stretched over a wheel by the sheriff. Refusing service to a ruffian was not permitted; deception was. I developed my skills. I would ply my clients with drink beforehand in the hope that a mere pantomime of the acts they desired would suffice. Often it did. Oafs like these were usually far gone and had known relatively little of women apart from the hand. Among the rough trade at this house, I one day recognized the "Count of Saint-Germain." The former Companion of Jesus Christ had been forced to flee Paris and intended to start a porcelain factory in Weesp, though his profligacy as a client of mine had surely shrunk his fortunes.

I remained in this position only long enough to pay off my bully. Afterward the gaming houses, where I worked as my own master, came as a relief; these girls were free to choose and never had to do anything against their wishes. My disfigurement prevented my attracting the most sought-after clients, but in these establishments even the less discerning men were at least God-fearing citizens. Most bought affection not of necessity but as a luxury, a refinement that made them appreciate us all the more. And the more a woman is appreciated, the more she esteems herself. I started to dress more smartly and took more pains with my health and appearance. Eating better, I grew rounder and fuller, and wealthier clients came as a result.

Meanwhile, I perfected my skills. It bears mentioning that I derived quite a few from *Dom Bougre,* the story of the gatekeeper of Chartreux; I had carried that book so long before I sold it there was not a single print with which I was not intimately acquainted. More and more I was able to furnish men pleasure without actual intercourse. It was my greatest satisfaction when, having scarcely been touched, they would depart contented.

In these better houses, one was also furnished "condoms." These sheaths, made from the intestines of cats or calves, were well known among surgeons—I had seen no one use them besides the anatomy professor. Now they were saving untold numbers of women from syphilis, as well as from unwanted children. Men were typically loath to wear them, though the madam of the house insisted. By a species of logic only the male mind could invent, it was assumed that a whore who requested this accommodation must be contaminated already, rather than wishing to save herself from subsequent infection. That is why it was important to encourage the gentleman first and then produce the sheath just when he had reached the stage at which he would have gladly put on a cap and bells for the sake of carrying on to the end.

One day as I was leaving one of these houses, a gentleman approached me. I had never seen him before. He wasn't a client. My suspicions were aroused, but he assured me that he desired only an opportunity to speak with me. Next to the Gentlemen's Guesthouse there was a coffeehouse, a perfectly respectable establishment, and there we passed a very pleasant two hours. He was erudite and spoke of books and philosophy, interests I'd been unable to pursue since coming to Amsterdam. (The city in general was not wanting in these refinements, but among my circle of acquaintance the life of the mind was mostly unlived.) In mid-conversation he stood up, made his apologies, and asked whether he might meet me again sometime. A worldly man, he paid me for my time without my asking and fled without revealing his name, which omission I found unexpectedly disappointing.

Two weeks later, he appeared again, this time in early evening, as I was entering the same house. He invited me to supper. I refused, being in need of the money I expected to earn that evening, but he promised I would profit by the invitation. The meal was exquisite, and again our conversation sparkled. At the end, shy and almost embarrassed, he handed me an envelope. It contained a charming tract he had described during our previous encounter. It concerned the imagination and was illustrated with plates showing a garden in full blossom and choked by weeds. I was moved to tears, I can't explain why. It was absurd to think that having come dry-eyed through so many horrors in this city I would be broken by this small kindness. Although I was afraid my show of sentiment would be misunderstood, I couldn't help myself.

"To surprise oneself in this way," he said, venturing an interpretation, "is perhaps to discover an unsuspected loneliness." He left me not only the gift but also, as promised, a handsome payment as well as a card bearing his name, Texeira, and an address on the Nieuwe Herengracht.

"If you care to go there, you will be well received."

A CARETAKER showed me to a small second-floor flat, comfortably furnished. I moved in early the next day. My benefactor visited several times a week, in return for which company he saw to my every worldly need. Turning my back on the public houses, I was able to start putting a little money aside. I felt a cautious optimism. The evenings I spent with Texeira, while never of the luster I had known in Bologna or Vincennes, were stimulating enough to revive my spirits and arouse my curiosity, which had been lulled without my realizing it.

I remember how, in the throes of my sickness, my fevered body had ceased all functions not immediately essential to survival, and I lay there alive but lifeless. So too had my mind reacted to my days of whoring—unfed, it had survived in dormancy. Now Texeira's humor and intelligence prodded it from its hibernation. Drowsily, ideas and convictions emerged from their cave, stretched, and gazed around in astonishment at the renewal of life. And so I looked forward to Texeira's visits with a happy expectation.

The happiness was short-lived.

There was a young girl called Danaë living in the flat below mine. She was being kept by a friend of Texeira's. We were cordial but not familiar with each other. One evening Texeira proposed that his friend bring Danaë to sup with us. It was not a success. The girl was fearful and loath to remain in any public place for long. She would jump at the approach of strangers. I imagined that Texeira's friend had terrorized her, and I inquired the next day, perhaps imprudently.

"Really, there's not a kinder soul in the world," she said, in the man's defense. "But of course there is the problem, as with Mr. Texeira." She spoke obliquely, and I, unwilling to appear ignorant and disadvantaged, would not ask forthrightly about something assumed to be understood. I let her continue talking in the hope of being offered a clue, but I was still equally ignorant at the end of the conversation, so before going upstairs I plucked up my courage and prodded her to make the matter plain.

"You know," she said. "That's what you get for being with a Jew."

THREE DAYS LATER, as I lay sleeping with my head on Texeira's chest, the constables entered my flat with an ax. They pulled us out of bed, manacled us roughly, and pushed us downstairs, where we were loaded into a cart. Danaë and her lover were lying there. Bystanders spat and jeered at us as if we were Gypsies, and we awaited trial for ten days with no clothes but the sheets we had hurriedly torn from the bed.

Aside from the freedom to live and practice their religion, Jews in Amsterdam, I would discover, were afforded few privileges. And since they were often wealthy enough to pay stiff fines, they were persecuted fanatically. Sexual relations with Christians were criminal offenses. Had Danaë not told me so, I would scarcely have believed it. It was true that I hadn't been aware of any Israelites in the brothels, but I'd heard that among its many forms of tolerance, Holland was most welcoming to them. Now I had cause to wonder whether Messieurs Voltaire and Descartes were aware of this contradiction when they praised Dutch liberty.

So it was by this path that I found myself in the spin house, where I would spend the next two years. The discipline was painful, the society of the women harsh. In the cells you had to fight for everything: a pallet, a chunk of bread, a chemise, a needle, sometimes even the right to catch a breath of fresh air at an open window. Disagreements were settled with bare hands and sometimes combs or scissors. The savagery of both the women and the patrons taught me more about the human soul than any philosopher would have wanted to know. It was soon apparent that any physical abnormality fed the bloodlust of the visitors. Only one woman regularly took my side. She was a gruff crone serving a long sentence for selling souls; this was how they described the offense of luring seamen into debt, thereby compelling them to return to sea as indentured servants. She had come to own many lives, which she would sell to the East India Company or some competitor. The work had accustomed her to dealing with sailors; whether out of compas-

sion toward me or resentment toward them, she regularly interceded when they abused me. Although she was usually surly
and sullen about her fate, she was the only prisoner who stood
up and embraced me when I was finally released.

I had had no knowledge of her grave illness, so when I
returned to the spin house as a spectator with Mr. Jamieson, I
hardly recognized her for all the chancres on her face, even as
she stared madly into mine.

Texeira had bought his way out of the rasp house and
planned to move to The Hague. He was so ashamed of the
ordeal I had suffered on his account that he couldn't face me. It
was just as well. I can now afford a bit of sympathy recalling
his plight, but at the time I was overflowing with the filthiest
recriminations. He offered to continue to support me with an
allowance, and I was in no position to refuse. With it I was able
to rent a flat on the Rusland with a room for Danaë, whose own
keeper had shown far less gallantry.

Danaë resumed her former work, giving me a fraction of
what she earned to cover her lodging. Later, she would take in a
friend of hers under the same conditions. Giovanna, who came
from Parma as well, had found success attracting better clients
by claiming to be the daughter of a Venetian nobleman. Only a
blind man without a nose could have believed such a lie, I would
have thought, but then deception depends mainly on the willingness of the deceived.

For my own part, there was no returning to that life for now.
My spirit had been exhausted by the openness of the Dutch.
Now the thoughtless looks of strangers were touching me as
they had not done before. At the slightest sidelong glance I
would flinch, as if the cruel chorus of the spin house were
about to erupt full-throated before me again. Even compassion

was disagreeable. I would answer it with a sharp tongue and later despise my coarse words and thin skin. The disfigurement I had so long confined to the outside now had an inner aspect, nurtured by fatigue and bitterness. I began to fear for my soul and saw that the only path to salvation was to subdue the part of me pulling me to perdition. I had imagined myself plucking out the right eye that was causing me to sin, little knowing that by resuming a habit I had left in Venice, I would make of my greatest frailty my greatest strength. Thereafter, I always went about veiled.

THIS IS MY LIFE. It happened this way. By telling the past, I attach myself to the present. It is not without misgiving that I lay bare my sordid history, and I would have preferred to remain silent no less than to have remained beautiful. But it proceeds. Without singleness of purpose I would have never begun, and my purpose is to make rationally comprehensible the decision I took and have yet to relate. To do that I shall need to tell the whole truth, even at the cost of any hope of sympathy. If I am to enjoy any compassion, let it be now. If the path has been foul, imagine where it leads.

3

IT SEEMS THAT *fate delights,* the actress on stage declaims, *in parting me from those who love me.*

The Amsterdam theater is quite full tonight, and we are pressed close together. As his ribs expand with breath, our sides touch. For minutes at a time we breathe to the same rhythm, like two who have always been together. As if I had crept into his bed one morning at Pasiano and never left it.

Then he slips away. A burst of laughter. Everyone there with us also finds the joke immensely witty. But I haven't been listening. He turns toward me, in mischievous complicity. I laugh heartily. It disrupts our rhythm. The laughter presses all the air out of his lungs. His shoulders shake. He catches his breath with a few quick gasps. One last chuckle, and we are together again. In and out. Out and in. His ribs against mine. Out. In. I think I can even feel his heartbeat now, or is it my own?

Where were you born, Fatima? she asks, her eyes wide with surprise for the far rows to see. *Cry over losing a man! Is that the fashion in these parts?*

I HAVE BEEN UNEASY all day, cursing the recklessness of ever having sent Giacomo that brazen challenge. A wager with love at stake! Did I ever imagine I could keep up the charade in his presence? My visit to the spin house two days ago has unmoored me. It brought the past before me again, at a moment when the future seemed more uncertain than ever. Heaven knows what perversity moved me to complicate the predicament. For to be truthful, I posed that grand challenge without any plan in mind.

Less than an hour before, I had been lacing myself into my finest dress and putting on a new veil of Indian gossamer when a fit of panic struck. I had the urge to flee from this ordeal, an urge no less powerful than had been my desperation to escape the seller of souls in the spin house. At a loss for an intuitive resolution, I tried to apply reason. What did I want? What could I do? I saw four paths.

1. Contrive a way to continue with Giacomo as if the years since our parting had never been. No sooner had I formed the thought than I disowned it as hopeless. My disappearance had changed him beyond recognition, myself no less. The Lucia and Giacomo of Pasiano were figures of history, two murdered innocents, their names usurped.

2. Reveal the simple truth, my true self, the reason for my apparent betrayal, my abject sorrow that the scheme, conceived for his sake, had miscarried so grotesquely. In the extreme instance, I would be obliged to reveal as well the cause of my shame and all our woe: my face, the very thing I had hoped to spare him. But with the chevalier so comfortably entrenched in cynical convictions and merry dalliance, he could show his heart to have been hardened even more by a refreshed contempt. Or would the sight of me soften him to the point of pity, which feeling would kill me faster?

3. Hold my tongue and not betray Galathée de Pompignac. Play the game of love a second time now as equals. I could come to know his true heart and plumb its depths, perhaps to see whether the woman I have become could win his heart and he hers. And then? To live ever after in this deception, in the shadow of a memory, ever blackened, of Lucia?

4. Flee a second time. Send him to the theater to find no one waiting, and earn for Galathée the contempt he imagines all women to deserve. His memory of Lucia would be no blacker. All would be as it was until the next conquered heart in his embrace would hear the honeyed song that always followed: his leitmotif, the dirge of the Italian serving girl.

I sat before the mirror, a paralytic in my finery. It was time to go. Among all the costs, calculated and uncalculated, of this ill-considered venture I could not reckon the smallest gain. Unless, of course, it were the few hours I might pass in Giacomo's proximity. I cursed my vain boast of victory in all events; the opposite was almost certainly inevitable. Only magic could save me now.

In that instant I remembered Zélide's counsel never to reflect on important decisions. When in doubt, withdraw in silence, close your eyes, and take a few deep breaths. Then do the first thing that comes to you. "Reason," she said, "offers us many possibilities at once. Intuition infallibly chooses the best."

I closed my eyes.

People are only capable of wanting one thing at a time.

WE KEEP OUR EYES on the stage, but I am oblivious to the drama, lost in the delight of sitting silently beside him, so naturally. His breathing quickens, a tension in his torso. Moving slightly, he leans toward me and with gentle assuredness lays an arm across the back of my seat and pulls me toward him.

"Do you see now," he whispers, "what misunderstandings are bred of?"

I purr my assent, as mysterious and omniscient as a sphinx, though at a perfect loss as to his meaning. As the tip of his nose brushes my earlobe I will my attention to the farce. Later, we will surely discuss it, and I cannot face him unarmed. Thank God, he sits up straight again, asks no more questions.

A veiled woman is standing on the boards. There is some confusion about her identity. I cast a sidelong glance at Giacomo.

He is evidently familiar with the piece. It is set in Turkey in the palace of the Mufti, who has fallen in love again with the woman he once cast out. According to the law of Muhammad, however, the Mufti cannot take her back until she has been married to another. The imam devises a solution wherein he engages an Italian, Harlequin, to marry Zaida and to reject her on the wedding night without having laid a finger on her, whereupon the Mufti will be free to make her his wife again. But this Harlequin, unbeknownst to his bride, happens to be the stranger who had saved her from drowning—and won her everlasting love. And so the sad couple spend their wedding night together, never undressing, waiting for morning to come. With Zaida veiled and Harlequin in darkness, they never realize how close to happiness they have come.

The audience has stopped laughing and is holding its breath. It all ends with a ballet as a Turkish woman sings:

> *Oh, lovers, listen and take heart,*
> *There is no foe you cannot beat;*
> *Miraculous love will take your part*
> *And conjure triumph from defeat.*

Later, in a *chambre séparée* at the City Inn, the door and walls of the small octagonal room hidden behind curtains of cobalt-blue moquette, Giacomo declares, "I am a disciple of the moment." A soft divan covered with orange cushions beckons shamelessly in the semidarkness. Although I give no sign of familiarity, I am no stranger to this room. Indeed, when I last supped here with a gentleman, I was served to him as dessert.

Giacomo laughs at the Mufti's absurd exertions to possess a woman.

"Contracts binding two people would be a fine idea if life were so immutable. But constantly it takes us by surprise. *Improvise,* it calls out to us. *Anticipate, vary!* One must be ever prepared to change course, don't you think? Eternal faithfulness is a creed for fools or for nuns walled into their cells."

Someone knocks on the door. When the waiter enters, Giacomo leans back and instructs him assuredly, making no pretense of awkwardness in this kind of rendezvous. His worldly sangfroid nettles me; I account myself to have been much happier with him silent beside me than holding forth in this way.

"And yet even you once hoped to marry," I say, once we are alone again.

"I?" he asks, in perfectly credible astonishment. "When might that have been?"

I am moved to end the charade here but persist in playing my part.

"It was undoubtedly a moment of uncharacteristic frailty. You told me about it yourself. Your very first girl, not far from Venice, if I recall. Yes, more to the point, you suffered some mischance when the festivities were canceled."

"I was a boy, and foolish. I learned never to fall into such a snare again."

"But could it be, sir, that the unfeeling wench still has you by the tail?"

"Perhaps she does. No one has ever loved me more. And yet such feeling did not stay her treacherous intent for a moment."

"You cannot possibly know that."

"Not knowing otherwise, I could not possibly hazard a second time the folly of complete surrender."

"So you have been faithful to no one since?"

"On the contrary, I have been faithful to all, without exception: to every love anew."

"But none for long."

"You seem very fond of this hobbyhorse, madame. Could it be that I have mistaken you? Your letter invited diversion, but you speak as one who has set her course for matrimony."

"Most definitely not, monsieur. I see no good in marriage, unless there is virtue in reducing talented men to husbands and accomplished women to their slaves."

A guinea hen is brought in. The headwaiter sharpens his knives, plants them in the flesh, and dissects the bird with a few deep slashes.

"No, my dear chevalier, my only fondness is for the stakes of our wager, which I expect to win. You would not deny me, in my pursuit of that prize, a bit more understanding of your *ars amoris* past and present, whereby to derive my strategy?"

"It has never changed, and if you would permit me to apply it without delay, I trust you would find them plain enough."

"Are you always in such haste to apply them?"

"Madame, I have not much time left in this city. With the new year I am expected in Paris to report to the government on my progress here." There is a brazen glint in his eye. "You would not deny me the happiness of reporting the success of *all* my ventures?"

"It shall be my greatest pleasure to furnish you assistance in such measure as I receive it. Now, monsieur, if you would suffer me to resume my honest inquiries: You claim you have never disappointed a woman. Assuming this premise, logic would suggest but two possibilities: Either your skill at love proved unequal to your skill at seduction—so the ladies were only too glad of seeing the end of both—"

A smug dismissive smile appears on his face.

"—or else you always made plain your intentions and reserve from the very beginning."

"Never less plain than your letter to me. Although I must say that I generally manage to frame the conditions less severely. But that is only fitting: To win a woman depends on a certain manner of expression. If a man but discloses his purpose softly enough, a woman will happily hear the opposite of what he has said. To convince her is a matter of time. By contrast, a woman desirous of a man's attentions need only whistle for him to come running like a dog in the street."

"Ah, there is no justice in this life." I laugh. "But perhaps you men would do better to cultivate feminine indifference."

"You do your sisters no justice. I have known countless women hungrier for love than any man."

"In your haste, you may have failed to notice that most take greater pleasure in the chase than the prize, while men find the pursuit a chore."

"Not at all. I delight no less in watering my garden than in gathering my flowers."

"Then we are well matched," I say, clinking glasses. "*Santé!*"

DURING THE MEAL, he tells me about some of his wildest adventures. I am struck less by the tale than the manner of its telling. It is invariably formal, suited to the warfare of wit one encounters in a salon. I wait endlessly, it seems, for his affect to soften and, all the while, try to remember the sound of our conversation in the days when I would creep onto his bed early in the morning with herbs I had picked for his tisane and he would rebuke me for the dirt falling off the roots onto his linens.

When he notices my mental absence, he begins to ask about my own life. He is hardly the first to have deduced that professing such interest is endearing to women. I tell him a few things that he cannot possibly connect with Pasiano. Trying to topple him from his rhetorical heights, I try to speak more directly, taking no pains to make my words sparkle. He changes tone accordingly.

"Have you never promised your heart to someone?"

"Of course," I reply. "Like you, I first gave it away far too young."

"And does he still possess it?"

We are midway through the second course, a veal pastry, as I start to doubt my ability to maintain the deception until the end.

"We lost track of each other."

"Such carelessness proves what I say. I can infer then that you agree everlasting love must sometimes capitulate to improvisation."

"As a practical matter, yes. Life goes on. But I still cherish the innocence of that first promise more than life itself, more than anything I have been told or seen proven since. In my darkest moments, it comforts me to know that once there was something that was indisputably genuine."

"A promise so genuine you couldn't keep it?"

At this my anger flares and my voice breaks as it hasn't since I was a girl. I pretend to be choking on some half-chewed bite of food and take several sips of wine, but I fear that even in this conduct I betray myself, slipping into the familiar gestures by which his brother recognized me in Venice. Though Francesco was always more observant than Giacomo, more sensitive perhaps as well. And so many years have passed. My voice is deeper, my shoulders lower, my figure fuller than it was.

Regaining my composure, I say, "The genuineness of a promise may be in the making as well as in the keeping. It is the only constant I have, you see: my faith that we both meant what we said."

"Then you have known more cause for happiness than I."

"And how could we have been anything but genuine in our innocence?"

My question is too direct, and he doesn't dare reply. I am at the limit of my restraint as well, so I am pleased that he pauses for a moment to fill my glass, and then his own, and cuts the pastry on his plate as he considers his reply.

"I don't believe I was ever innocent. I know that in my youth I upheld a number of values that were discredited in time by experience."

"I'm so sorry."

"Why?" he sneers. "It's hardly your fault."

I have to bite my lip. He can't possibly see this through the veil, but he surmises.

"It's no great tragedy, Gala."

That name. It is the first time he has addressed me by it. It sounds sweet on his lips. Still, I would rather hear the former one.

"Surely you don't still cherish those things you cherished as a girl?" he says, laying his hand on mine for a moment. "To come of age is to make one's peace with reality."

I would like to respond in a manner befitting a worthy adversary, but I am unexpectedly struck dumb. Trying to defeat him by devious means of forced recollection, I find it is I who have been lured onto those treacherous shoals of memory. Are my feelings tonight really so different from what I felt then? When I departed Pasiano to go off into the world, I thought I was leaving Giacomo behind. Now, it seems, I was the one forsaken.

"When Marco Polo returned from the Great Khan, he told of holy men who so revered life that they used fagots to sweep the ground before their feet. Only with the assurance of not trampling a single living thing would they take a step forward. They died without harming so much as a fly—but they never got very far from home," he points out.

"Maybe they began where they wished to be," I say.

"High standards are a wonderful starting point. They may even save us from follies in our youth. But people who cling to such standards afterward deter their progress. We can't possibly live up to them and live life at the same time."

"So you trample all over them."

"They fall by the wayside. That's unavoidable. They die, one after another, like brave soldiers sent into the breach. Anyone who would avoid this should seek refuge in a cloister. There you won't hurt anyone, and no one will hurt you, and you can believe the things your parents told you until the end of your days."

"Such a dark heart!"

"Quite the contrary, madame, it is bathed in the light of truth. It is the darkness of youth I have abjured, in which things appear not as they truly are."

"So you would renounce the tender feelings of your youth as shadows and specters?" I exclaim, suddenly fierce. "And what of the poor fools who have trusted you, were they likewise unsubstantial?" I am aware of slipping out of character. He looks at me quietly, as if searching for the source of such indignation.

"It is always heartbreaking to part with one's illusions," he says sympathetically, "but I have always discerned a great beauty in that sorrow."

"Speak plainly!"

"We mourn the death of someone we love, but at the same time that grief awakens us more fully to being ourselves alive. We resolve henceforth to meet what we have left of this miracle even more intensely. In just this way, we lament the loss of every fond ideal but cling all the more mightily to what remains."

"And that is?"

"Not as lofty but more reliable. Less fantastical and more reasonable. We leave our state of nature farther and farther behind and develop from emotional creatures into rational beings. This is the beauty I feel in the loss of illusion: The pain is proof that we have taken another step on the path."

"And the creature underfoot that knows nothing higher than its nature?"

Giacomo shrugs. "Alas!" He claps his hands together, as if crushing some unsuspecting bug. "Don't look so surprised, *ma chère*. Life has shaped you in the same way, not by gentle molding but with the hard blows of a sharp chisel."

I shiver. Taking it for a sign, he stands up and puts an arm around me. I let him have his way.

WITH MOST of the candles burned down, the room is darkening. I will myself to fix my mind on each caress, but my concentration fails me. I have imagined this moment for years, in hundreds of different ways, from drunken to solemn. Now living it, the act seems less real than my dreams. I cannot surrender to it. His lips on my throat. I groan softly, as I am dutifully accustomed, but I don't feel him; I don't feel that now it is *he*, anymore than it is *I*. The masquerade of this evening has led my body to stray from my mind. Giacomo notices and hesitates for a moment before gently continuing. He runs his nails down my back. *This is* Giacomo, I tell myself, *his hand, his waist. Think of it! You had years ago abandoned all hope of him.* And now? I put his hands on my breasts. I raise my veil slightly to let him kiss me. His lips brush mine. I feel his breath on my throat.

Then he stops.

"I'm sorry." He sits up straight. "This is unforgivable, I know, but I can't do it. It's impossible. Not tonight. Forgive me, for God's sake."

I straighten my garments and mumble something frivolous, but this does not produce a lightening of spirits.

Giacomo hides his face in his hands. He gasps for breath. His suffering is palpable. Now I am the one to lay my arm around his shoulders, but he shrugs me off and stands up as if to escape me.

I am mystified, imagining the worst of possibilities in turn and then all at once. He has discovered my identity after all. He has surmised my disfigurement. Perhaps, in the excitement of this transport, I have exposed myself as a whore and repelled him. Perhaps, God forbid, he has been stricken with an apoplexy.

His face in the light of the last candle, he bends forward, laying a hand on the table. With the other he pours a glass of wine, then gulps it down straightaway. I take his hand and stroke it, as one would console a child who's fallen, still without comprehension.

"Forgive me," he says at last. "I underestimated the effect of our exchange."

I apologize, without knowing whether I have given cause for distress.

"I had not for years been so completely delivered to the distant past." His swagger crumbles as he sinks into his chair. He shakes his head ruefully. "Believe me, madame, I do not deceive you when I say I would love you well, body and soul. But my thoughts have carried me from this room to a place in which I am not eager to dwell. You see, I must confess it: I have not dispelled all the shadows of my youth."

I stiffen. *He has divined everything!* I say to myself. But how could that be?

"If you would grant me a chance to see you again, Galathée, though I've done nothing to deserve your forbearance, I will prove myself faithful to my word and more," he says remorsefully. "But as for tonight, I must take my leave of you."

I take his face in my hands, uncertain whether to speak with reproach or pity, and ask simply, "What has come over you?"

"Our wager. Our exchange. You've set me doubting. The things you ask. The things you suggest." He turns away again, as if trying to pluck up courage to continue. "What if I really *have* hurt someone?"

"By your own report there is no evidence of your having done the least harm, not even the intention," I say soothingly.

"None, I swear it. But," he says, now almost choked with emotion, "the proof is hardly beyond dispute. If I cannot be certain of having done injury to no one in the past, who can assure me that I will do no harm henceforth?"

Neither of us says another word. I know what I must do. I stand before him and undress, removing everything except my veil. I unbutton his breeches and find behind the flaps that his manhood is not nearly as depressed as his spirits. I take hold of him and kiss him until nature revives his initiative. He throws himself upon me, biting, growling. We roll over across the floor in feral excitation. I let him pin me down, certain of rising up all the more powerfully after. He does the same. Without time for thought or thought for time, my lover has to grab the legs of the divan to steady himself. I mount him as I have mounted nothing with such guileless pleasure but the horses of Pasiano. His eyes drain of thought, his every anxiety forgotten. For a moment I feel a kind of pride at being the agent of his deliverance. And then another thought dawns.

What artful wickedness! A man so expert in the ways of love knows the most subtle of strategies: to think like the women he would conquer. A weapon for which there is no defense. And for all my experience, he used it without effort to carve me like the guinea hen on the table. What surer way for a man to win a woman than to reveal himself in possession of an unexpected tenderness of feeling. Giacomo is so sophisticated at this game, he knows that pity can make a woman's fire rage. Of course he does. By feigning doubt, he let vulnerability shine through his formal conversation. His sudden anxiety was but a pretense to gain my sympathy—that's right, a device to arouse me by melting my heart—hoping I would encourage him by my initiative, just as I, fool that I am, now am doing.

I see it all in a flash. But the thought is stillborn. It comes too late to turn the tide of feeling. Under my thighs I feel his muscles contract. I feel his life in mine. I'm taken completely by this pleasure and, with unfeigned excitement, ride him out.

4

I WAS SEEKING DISTANCE. When, shortly after my release from the spin house, I lowered a veil before the world, it was by this illusion that I attempted to create the impression of being at some remove from everything. The first one I bought was of a fabric from Gaza. The mesh was not especially fine, but the cloth was dotted with skillfully embroidered ladybirds obscuring the inward view without reducing what I could see. While Venetians spend a whole season going about in every manner of mask, luxuriating in their varieties of disguise, in Amsterdam this presentation was exceptional. Noble ladies occasionally wore veils, but only at the theater or a ball. On the street you might see a masked person in a carriage, but never simply walking by a canal.

My first steps outside in this state of concealment did not come naturally. At home in front of the mirror, I put on and removed the veil several times, trying to imagine the impression it would make upon someone seeing it for the first time. In truth I hesitated even more than I had before first walking the streets. It was surprising to find it easier to go out as a whore than as a lady. But that's the way of it: It takes more courage to cover yourself than it does to lay yourself bare, perhaps because in some sense the former condition is more revealing.

I went out for my first stroll at twilight, resolving to remain in the shadows and not stray far from home. I was immediately remarked upon—a familiar experience; the veil was not less conspicuous than my scars—but the attention I attracted was different. There was neither evident repulsion nor a sign of its opposite, pity. No fewer people stared, but their gazes affected me less profoundly. I saw the puzzled expression with which one might countenance any number of eccentricities—and Holland had its eccentrics, to be sure—but that was all. I decided to accost someone, a complete stranger, to ask directions, even though I was but two streets away from home. The gentleman removed his hat and calmly pointed out the route I should take. I then commented on the weather. We struck up a conversation and walked alongside each other for a minute or two. When our ways parted, we said a cordial goodbye. I was overwhelmed by such joy that just a quarter of an hour later I couldn't remember a word of what was said. I felt free as I never had before in this country. And again the paradox, fathomable only to those accustomed to being despised at first glance: I felt as though I were finally at liberty to reveal myself, as if my character had become discernible only after I had hidden my face. Suffice it to say that I considered myself presentable only when I was invisible.

"Hey, Lady Muck!" A sudden yowl went up. My heart sank. My new self-confidence, frail as a sparrow's bones, shattered with the first blow. Blood rushed through my veins. As usual I surveyed all routes of escape at a single glance and took the measure of my adversaries, a gang of overgrown louts. Shoulder to shoulder they approached me. One led the way, amusing the others with a mockery of my uneasy gait. I slowed my pace, estimating my chances for successful flight. They were drunk, typically an advantage for me, but their spirits were high, and fleeing would encourage them. They would not fail to give chase if their prey bolted.

"The last head I saw in a net like that was a mackerel!" one of them jeered.

"Now you mention it," another agreed, "the air *is* a bit fishy around here."

As he gathered his laurels, I realized that their mockery was directed not at my person but at my dress. They had no way of seeing my imperfection and would have similarly abused the first unescorted woman to cross their path. I decided to walk on, wary but determined. For a moment they made as if to block my way and do to me what they might to a mackerel, but when I gave no sign of being cowed, their ranks parted and they let me through.

"Hey, Reaper, they're burying the baron over there!" one of them called out behind me, the rest hurling a few coarse words but nothing more.

I went home that day strangely fortified, a hymn of victory sounding in my mind. The barbs that that had been slung at me these years since I left home had been but absurd curses and mockery, but their want of truth never softened their sting. These, however, could be brushed off without pain. To have been so long judged by an outer aspect of which I had not the least control had been a torment heretofore unacknowledged. Abused though I might continue to be, it would hereafter be on account of a countenance I had chosen, and the fine veil became as chain mail when cruelties were flung at me.

In the weeks that followed I began to build a small collection. Whenever I heard that a ship had put into port with fabrics from the East, I would go straight to the quay to make my selection. Behind the Montelbaan Tower, I found a seamstress who sewed veils according to my precise wishes. Together we contrived cunning designs wherein closely woven and decorative pieces were placed so as to obstruct the view of my scars while the sheer parts hung before my eyes and undamaged skin. In a short period, I acquired a variety of distinct guises, enough to suit a range of moods. How much more agreeable it was to elect my manner of difference from others.

My veil was of unexpected benefit in my profession. Men like to guess. They would rather search than have the certain truth put before them. And just as the outline of a firm breast beneath a snug bodice is more alluring than the unclothed part, the veil was more attractive than the fairest face, allowing each man to imagine after his taste or simply to avail himself of that phantasm of guiltless lust, a faceless woman.

The suggestiveness of my veil seemed irresistible. People suspected a mystery, and the news spread. I no longer passed a single night without an admirer, and their numbers included no few representatives of the better classes. The world seemed to have been turned on its head: Instead of waiting to be chosen, I was now forced every night to decline a few suitors. I chose the clean-bodied and the well formed, the prosperous and the modestly handsome, and by degrees my work became more pleasant, sometimes to the point of not seeming to be an objectionable necessity. The improvement was circular: As I found more enjoyment, so did my visitors, who rewarded me in gratifying proportion. I raised my rates, cautiously at first, afraid of overestimating what the market would bear, but they grew more and more boldly exorbitant as I observed that the quality of men I received, far from suffering, improved as my attentions grew more dear.

This progress continued until the experience of my company became a matter of pride among the city's wealthy and aristocratic men. I do not boast in reporting that I began a kind of fashion, for around this time so-called Salomes were introduced in several of the better bordellos. These were dancers who enticed visitors by affecting Oriental manners and wrapping their faces in thin veils. The error these amateurs made without exception was to accept payment for the removal of their veils. No matter how plaintively this favor was sought, I would never indulge it. Each new lover would invariably ask, often imagining that it was simply a matter of offering the right price. But the more resolute my refusals, the greater and more appealing the mystery, and in each man's efforts to dispel it I took the measure of his means to pay for every other sort of service.

It was not long before I reached a time of happy consolidation of my affairs, restricting myself to a few regulars, gentlemen of quality with whom I felt at ease. Jan Rijgerbos was one, along with Egbert Trip and several other city councilors. Allocating each man his own regular evening in the week, I watched as each tried to divine the days of the others, whom he would strive in his turn to outdo in my affections. In the unusual event that a man might be unable to present himself on his day, the evening was never wasted, for I had also established arrangements with a few infrequent visitors to the city, men loath to pass even a night here in solitude. In this category there was the Spanish envoy, for instance, and, before his business had brought him here for an indefinite time, the merchant Jamieson.

Though my work was never anything but a matter of vital necessity, I began for the first time in years to feel a happy self-sufficiency. I had everything requisite to a pleasant—indeed, a comfortable—life. At the same time, I was free of the obligations of a kept woman, who is perforce under a yoke, even if it is as light as poor kindly Texeira's. Now I could refuse anyone, and did nothing involuntarily. Such free will was a natural tonic for my self-esteem.

In this vale my tears were joyful. It came to seem unimaginable how I had abased myself for a measure of acceptance, when with a simple change, as if by magic, I had been placed in the tyrannical seat of refusal; unimaginable seemed my former suffering when a reprobate, grimy and reeking, summed me up with a glance and walked on disdainfully to the next in line, compelling a further abasement of my person and cost.

I could deceive myself that it was a price I paid to survive. But the transmutation of my circumstances in a single stroke made plain that this was untrue. Such faces and bodies as I had suffered to know would have made death by starvation seem like everlasting deliverance. I was, if I'm honest, glad of being used. It was not to preserve life that I was moved to those vile labors; the meanest of honest work would have been sufficient to that end. It was rather to recover that sense with which I had but brief honorable acquaintance, and which is the last possession a woman can bear to part with: the intoxicating justification of being desired. It was this abject consolation I had been searching for among the low and the rough. It had been that way ever since I had let old Antonio, the Count of Montereale, have his way with me.

In the heady satisfaction of being instantly re-formed, of being seen almost as if I were the girl so long lost to me, there was one insight that eluded me still, though on reflection it is perfectly plain: It was in fact I, not the suitors or idle gawkers, who had learned to see Lucia without prejudice! At last, I had stopped imagining myself in the gaze of others. This was the reason for my success, both privately and at my labors. My happiness no longer dependent on what strangers tossed my way, I now found enough of myself to share it out. And so the mask I had put on to distance myself actually brought me closer to other people.

. . .

WITHIN THE SWIRL of new impressions, I caught glimpses of a truth I could not quite place, like the feeling we sometimes get at a bedside where a loved one lies dying or giving birth: a sense of one thing overshadowing all else, allowing us, if only for a single moment, to look our existence squarely in the eye. Like copper atoms in a boiling flask, these impressions remained volatile and nonreactive. To divine in them the key to my future, I would need an antimony, a medium that would cause the precipitation of all the dust that had been stirred up. This clarity would come to me only through Giacomo.

5

"It really is incomprehensible." He laughs, as I incline languorously upon his chest following our pleasure. "Can you imagine some people call this heavenly gift a sin and repent of it?" He rolls me aside and steps out of bed—to dress himself and depart, I assume, but nothing could be farther from his mind. As if the job is only half done, he sits down on the edge of the divan, crosses his legs, and lays my feet in his lap, rubbing them with a gentle pressure that prolongs the last pangs of my longing until it surges again.

"What aliens to this world such people must be."

We spend the whole of that first night in each other's arms. And in the days that follow, the last ones of that year, he hardly leaves my side. I bask in his attention like a pilgrim luxuriating in a healing spring, following a long journey.

It is true that Giacomo proves an exceptional lover, tender and exuberant at once. His candid devotion to his own pleasure and the refinement with which he seeks it are refreshing. He believes, and I have come to agree, that the greatest heights of one's own rapture can be reached only in synchrony with another's. And so his unfailing attention, and the impression he gives of being in the presence of feminine perfection, is vital to his hedonism. Only the most embittered cynic could object. It is a happy illusion one is offered, curiously undiminished by his frank talk of other conquests. Giacomo's talent is to take tales another man would share only at a tavern and make of them an element of his insuperable charm *au lit*. When our stormy thrashing has subsided, and we lie motionless side by side, he discloses his most intimate adventures. Sometimes he even asks me how in his place I would have negotiated a particular seduction or how a woman might react to a certain piquancy proposed in plain terms.

The astonishing fact is that I feel no offense or jealousy at these moments. For this immunity from darker feeling, I can credit one fact: I am with Giacomo on terms of perfect equality, a condition I have known with no other man. We are like children, as mischievous as we are innocent, giggling complicitously about the adult matters we discover in our play. *This is the way things are*, he seems to say. *These are my pranks. I recount them to aver that I have met my match.*

Such parity is an infallible aphrodisiac, but for a lasting effect both parties must swallow it.

"FOURTEEN!" I LAUGH.

On New Year's Eve, our third night together, Giacomo reveals a dilemma concerning a girl he has mentioned several times before. He has recently succeeded in making a great impression on her with his magic squares and pyramids. It is one of the stories he tells to entertain me and to demonstrate that I enjoy his absolute trust. He finds this Hester enchanting. She is the daughter of Hendrik Hooft, an Amsterdam alderman.

Giacomo has been cultivating her affections for some time but hasn't dared to press his case too far on account of her tender age.

"She will mourn the loss of your attention, and, should she discover that you haven't simply fallen into one of the canals, she will surely curse the shrew who has turned your gaze from her."

"I told her I didn't dare see her every day, as her eyes were devouring my soul."

"And how was this sophistry received?"

"Not at all." He shook his head with admiration. "Only fourteen and already so astute!"

"For a girl, the fourteenth is a year of great clarity," I observe, as dispassionately as I can. "It is a moment of great impressions and deep tracks, and she is never farther ahead of a boy of the same years. At the same time, her innate clairvoyance has not yet been overshadowed by the world. Yes, it's a time when everything she experiences will remain with her for the rest of her life. Please be careful. It is a dangerous age, fourteen."

Whether insensible of my earnest admonitions or unwilling to be restrained by them, he lets my words pass without comment. He relates a daring feat by which he convinced the child of the supernatural attributes of his oracle. She had doubted his cabalistic skills and challenged him to divine from his numbers something that no one but she could know.

"In the dimple on her chin, Hester has a charming black mole," he says. "It is very small but rises slightly above the surface. Like everyone with some knowledge of anatomy and physiology, I know that every visible aspect of the face—length, structure, color and thickness of hair growth, the fullness and shape of the lips—is reflected in the characteristics of other bodily parts that respectable girls generally keep hidden."

"A brilliant hypothesis," I mock, but Giacomo holds fast to

his belief in this old wives' tale and teases me that in my case there is proof that the converse is also true: He is content that I continue to wear my veil because my body has already disclosed to him the character of my face.

"Assured as I was of my reasoning," he continues earnestly, "I wanted to offer Hester a particularly startling proof of my oracle's powers: 'O chaste beauty, not a soul knows that on the most secret part of your body, that place vouchsafed to love alone, you have a little mole exactly like the one on your chin.' She was astonished, not at the truth of my pronouncement but at the news that there were any moles on her nether body. So innocent! She permitted me to seek it with my hand, and, seeing doubt in my eyes, she let me have a look."

"And?"

"It was there, of course. No larger than a millet seed, but there still. She allowed me to kiss it until I was breathless."

"And there relented?"

"Alas."

His story has stirred him, and as he kisses my neck I cannot keep from entertaining a thought of his venturing with me the same investigation.

"What else could I do? Fourteen!"

"The same age presented no impediment on a prior occasion."

"In fact it did. Fortunately *you* have left that troublesome tender age behind."

"True," I concede, "but nowadays my good opinion is withheld from all but the most extraordinary men."

He takes this for encouragement and I offer no resistance, though I submit without the earlier relish. As he loses himself in me, I feel our every movement rocking me awake as if the bliss of the last few days has been but a dream.

I AM NOT the kind of woman who fails to see men as they are and turns away from them when they dash her hopes. Without expectation there is no disillusionment. This might sound like bitterness to the novice at love, but it consoles the experienced heart. People are afraid to adjust their ideals. They would sooner overreach than accept a toehold when it has been offered. That's something I have never understood. You can spend your whole life with your mouth watering, watching a feast you shall never join, wallowing in youthful longings, finally to die with your ideals intact. But what are they worth if you never once notice the miracle that takes place every day, when your empty stomach transforms the cast-off crusts of bread into the most sublime delicacy? Anyone can hope for abundance, but only with imagination can one find splendors in deficiency!

And so his story of Hester was as salutary as it was irksome. Nothing tempers my dreams more surely than reality.

"MY ONLY LINGERING WORRY," he adds, "is that the girl will ascribe my divination to what one day she will surely discover to be an ordinary fact of nature."

"I wouldn't worry," I reassure him, our bodies still fused together. "I myself had never heard it suggested before today."

In moments like this I can already feel myself in retreat from him, a growing distance through which my heart steps back from Giacomo, without sorrow, for a better view.

"These anxieties tear at me in every instance," he says. "With you too! The fear that I might lose your good opinion and your trust." He ceases his exertions and then, sitting up, says without irony or guile, "It corrodes the soul to love someone and realize that you are not worthy of her."

He might be referring to me, perhaps to Hester. It doesn't really matter. "So why persist? If you really believe you don't deserve her, why not let her go?"

He looks at me, incredulous. "In view of the gates of paradise?" The thought of not plucking a prize that is within his reach dawns on him as such an absurdity that his seriousness is dispelled and his playfulness returns. He crawls over the bed and, kneeling before me, pries apart my legs with gentle fingers.

"See paradise and renounce it?" Shaking his head, he disappears between my thighs. "Who but a fool would be so blasphemous?"

The sign I have been waiting for.

I REMAIN GIACOMO'S LOVER for a whole week, until his departure for Paris on the fifth day of the new year. Only once is our pleasure interrupted, on the Thursday afternoon when Jamieson appears at my door for our regular appointment. The past few days and nights have merged together so completely that I have lost track of time and am totally unprepared. I make myself as presentable as I can, but my efforts do not persuade Jamieson that I have remembered our engagement. When I let him in, I give the impression of being a sack just fished out of the harbor.

"I'm sorry," I mumble. "The grippe. I've been ill."

"You poor dear," he says, kissing me before climbing the stairs to the parlor room as always. There, to his surprise, he finds Monsieur le Chevalier de Seingalt, resplendent in his Parisian silk, sipping a cup of tea. Giacomo's performance is more credible than my own; slumped in a chair like a pile of linens gathered for washing, he has the air of having spent far too long visiting this invalid.

"Ah, Mr. Jamieson!" He leaps up, seizing his hand warmly.

"At last, some distraction!" Then, seizing the teapot that hasn't been used for days, he hands it to me as if it has just gone cold and suggests putting on a fresh kettle for the guest. Here is a man superbly practiced at delivering himself from every kind of awkwardness.

Downstairs in the kitchen, I now have a moment to arrange myself properly and, as Giacomo chats amiably with Jamieson, I climb the back staircase to remove all traces of our activity in the bedroom.

"But what do you have against the New World?" I hear Jamieson ask, as I return with the steaming pot. "Are you so afraid of the future?"

"Not in Europe. On the contrary. We have turned toward the light and are on the eve of a new era of reason and equality."

"Aren't the Americas the perfect laboratory in which to test these new theories of yours, a virgin territory unmolested and unencumbered by the past?"

"But, sir, our theories have issued from that very past. We have charted and classified it and from it shaped—defined—every new idea. We owe to it our mastery of our innate nature. Our new tree has only lately come into bud and is as yet too delicate to be uprooted from its native soil and transplanted. Your continent is in a state of chaos. It has no civilization and is especially lacking in the tolerance we have won here in Europe through so much struggle."

"I believe," I say, while pouring the tea, "that Monsieur de Seingalt's judgment would be rather less harsh if America had fallen into French hands."

"That battle is not yet over," Giacomo says, without a trace of irony. "But as things stand, you will have to start from scratch and reinvent civilization."

"Never fear," says Jamieson, refusing for my sake to rise to the bait. "A new country with new possibilities and borders that are still expanding has at least one advantage over you: We are driven by hope."

"Yes, I've heard your compatriots talk about it before. It is a completely irrational optimism, without root in reason and, unlike ours, all in the heart. It is self-sustaining enthusiasm, immune to both fact and argument."

"Just the kind I always rely on," I interject frivolously to restore the former amity, then steer the conversation into calmer waters. Giacomo lingers for a half hour longer before declaring his wish to tire the convalescent no more. The gentlemen quit my house together, parting ways at the door.

"You have seen so much of the world already," Jamieson says, by way of farewell. "Perhaps you, of all people, should honor us with a visit, Monsieur de Seingalt. Then you could see the unlimited possibilities with your own eyes. You seem to me the kind of man who would not hesitate to seize hold of anything that might prove opportune."

"I should not wish to take advantage of your countrymen's callowness in affairs, sir," Giacomo replies, seeming to have missed the insult. Meanwhile, he winks at me as a sign that he will reappear on my doorstep after a brief stroll. "It bears no consideration, neither the land nor the people. You will never see me there, not as long as I live and breathe; you may rest assured of that."

TO SEE THEMSELVES, people look in a mirror. If they detect something unexpected, they incline toward the glass to inspect the irregularity more closely. For my part, I see myself more clearly from a distance.

While being exhibited in the anatomical theater, I needed to dissociate my thoughts from my naked body and the cadaver that was being dissected beside me. In such depths, the soul takes wing. Often enough I would rediscover myself on one of the benches in the back row of the lecture theater, following the lesson with the other students. I would watch the professor lay bare the sinews and sever them before setting them on the back of the anonymous living model. I would study the young woman dispassionately and at my leisure. These were useful exercises.

Later, in the ghastliest of situations, as I was undressing for one man after another, letting each watch and touch me according to his desire, this detachment would prove a gift. I could—as in the anatomical theater—observe the entire scene, in which I was the principal player, as if from a distance, as if in the company of the gods looking down at the young woman receiving the lessons they had contrived for her.

During my last days in Giacomo's arms, I caught my thoughts wandering in that same direction. I struggled to drag myself back, to be present to him, but the temptation to stand and watch was irresistible! From a distance, I had the most agreeable view of my delight in Fortune's having given me this occasion to relish the love it had taken from me cruelly so long ago.

CONTEMPLATING WHAT is to follow and what has been left unsaid, I am never more certain that love is much more safely observed than experienced. I yearn to bring things to a happy end, but I don't know how. One plan after the other rises in my mind as our limbs mingle, more frantically and avidly as time grows short. Then suddenly I see a way. I cry out, as lovers do, and gasp for air.

The answer comes from the farthest row of the lecture theater, high above the bed in which love is dissected. My first separation from Giacomo decided the course of my life. The time for a second farewell is at hand. And if my plan succeeds, if I can find the strength, a third and final parting is still to come.

On the eve of his departure, our last night together, the shortness of time does not enrich the dwindling hours. What pleasure we take is deliberate, all attempts at surrender defeated. With more desperation than joy, we grasp at each successive moment, hoping vainly it will offer up something more than the last. We cling, panicked, like the boy whom we learned had drowned trying to cross the frozen river IJssel too late this winter. Had he stopped, someone might have been able to rescue him, but, heedless of the voices calling out to him, he heard only the cracking of the floes beneath his feet, which spurred him on recklessly to the unreachable far bank.

In the morning, Giacomo leaves my bed without waking me and hurries off to his lodgings to pack his belongings and dispatch them to the post office. I meet him there at ten o'clock, just as the coach is about to depart. If it is unavoidable, then let it be sharp. The other passengers have already boarded and are anxious for the journey to begin.

"And?" he asks, with one foot on the step. "Any regrets? Have I won our wager?"

"It pains me to say I *am* sorry to see you go."

"I told you at the start I would not stay long."

"That is true."

"And I will certainly return, perhaps in spring. You will be here, won't you, waiting for me?"

Those sentences! I have to fortify myself to stand firm. It seems as if I recognize them word for word, although it may be a trick of memory. He mounts the coach. The other passengers' faces register relief. I manage a laugh and raise an admonishing finger playfully.

"Shame on you, daring to ask a thing like that."

"Evidently the answer requires more courage than the question, because you don't dare give it."

"I can promise you nothing. I would not make the same mistake as your Lucia."

He stares at me dumbstruck as the door is closed.

"Your first love, the one who deceived you so cruelly," I say, by way of explanation. I betray no awareness of having made a faux pas and try to change the subject. "You really should know better. I could be overtaken by a sudden urge for travel, perhaps to some remote place. And you would be left to despise me. No, no promises!"

As the coach driver gives the reins a shake, Giacomo's expression is that of a sailor who has just seen a ghost ship. I turn to make my way home. Inclined toward me from the open window, he calls out.

"Her name?"

"Pardon?"

"Surely I never spoke that name. Not in your presence. How do you know Lucia's name?"

With a decisive lash, the team jolts forward. The undercarriage creaks. The wheels rattle on the cobbles.

"It's quite simple," I call out, waving goodbye. "I know this Lucia of yours!"

6

I HAVE KNOWN HUNGER. Sometimes in foul weather, with the fleet trapped before Texel for a week or two, there weren't men enough for all the women walking the streets of the capital. You could spend days wandering and find no one seeking the use of you. I remember this struggle in three phases, of which the first is a gnawing in the stomach, when worry soon gives way to panic and your body hungers for everything it sees.

Then want becomes desperation. There is no place for fear or hesitation. Like a savage you forage, scraping up things only half edible. You snatch whatever you can find and pop it into your mouth. You take without thought.

But Nature shows itself to be ultimately merciful. In the face of death, a wave of indifference washes over you. You rise above it and let yourself be carried along. A blissful peace overcomes you. Instead of worrying about life, you look ahead. There is no wish to have, no wish to take, or even to hold on. The beleaguered mind lowers its defenses. It opens up. It begins to hallucinate. The feeling is an addiction, so much so that you are hardly grateful when you happen to be rescued. The abandonment of calculation, the absence of choice: Only in this submission, with limbs relaxed and trusting to the water, do the drowning pose no danger of pulling their would-be rescuers down with them. In this state they are most easily saved.

For me, so it was with love. For a long time I had believed that to survive I had to cling to it with all my might.

GIACOMO WAS BACK from Paris before two months had passed, even before the thaw had set in. I was frightened at the prospect of a reunion. I was afraid that it would weaken my resolve and cause me at the fateful moment to shrink from the formidable test that lay ahead. On the other hand, my plan had so ripened by then that I longed to see it enacted, whatever forces it might unleash.

Still traveling as the Chevalier de Seingalt, he had moved into the Second Bible in the Warmoesstraat, where he asked to receive me in his rooms that evening, if not to visit me at home. His stated intention was to return to where we had been on the eve of his departure. But I knew that the moment his skin brushed mine, the weeks of determination laid on like so many coats of paint would bubble and crack. Indeed a single word, whispered in my ear, would for all I knew have made it almost impossible for me to persevere.

No, Giacomo and I would have to remain apart until our final meeting, just as prospective combatants are kept apart, lest the sight of one stir the least pity in the other.

Accordingly, I answered his invitation with delight at the arrival of such a dear friend in the city but with regret at being otherwise engaged for the evening. I went out that night with Jamieson as arranged.

The American wanted to celebrate the highly profitable conclusion of his business on the stock exchange and his acquisition of a ten-year monopoly in the Low Countries. He gave me a necklace of black pearls, which, despite his rough clumsy fingers, he insisted on fastening himself. I was moved at the care he took not to unsettle my veil. We were alone, and of course he had seen all there was to see of my imperfection in the spin house. So to indulge my continued attachment to this garb betrayed an unexpected tenderness. I accepted his gift gladly, knowing it was time for him to take his profits back to New York and resume control of his trading company. He would be sailing as soon as the harbor was free of ice. I had anticipated for some weeks the loss of a substantial source of regular income with no prospect of a replacement. It was almost certain that I would have to surrender my flat for an even humbler one, but now, at least, I could fend off impoverishment for a while longer. Jamieson's pearls would be marched straightaway to the pawnbroker.

I was still making quite a show of my gratitude when a messenger arrived with another letter from Giacomo. He pressed for a reunion at the soonest opportunity, when, he hoped, I would solve a riddle I had left him with on his departure. I put the letter away as soon as I had read it, giving Jamieson his due attention once more. He, however, was too perceptive for a man. Noticing my disquiet and seeing that my thoughts were elsewhere, he let me know with a light touch that a more strenuous show of thanks was not required. He lingered just long enough to see that I had recovered my serenity and left me to an early bed.

I DIDN'T SLEEP AT ALL. I took my grandfather's pendant out from where I had packed it away at the bottom of my valise and sat up all night holding it. I refused to be deterred by what I had read. For the first time in many years I looked beyond my reflection and prayed to Santa Lucia. I asked for courage, superhuman courage, of the kind that had enabled her to pluck out her own eyes rather than succumb to the sight of her lover and betray her calling. I stirred myself into such an ecstasy that, for a few moments, I thought I could feel her agony in my own nerves. Thank God my good sense returned in time, and with it my long-held contempt for women who make pointless sacrifices. I sat down at my writing table and did what needed to be done, strengthened by the knowledge that I would have my reward in this life, not the next.

My beloved de Seingalt, chevalier,

Alas. Urgent affairs demand that I depart at once for Utrecht, where I am likely to remain only briefly before continuing on to Cologne and possibly farther points. Fate, it would seem, has not smiled upon the reunion we have both been anticipating so keenly. I have no wish, however, to keep from you the answer to the riddle you say has plagued you since our parting. I presume it concerns the result of our wager. As you no doubt recall, it involved two challenges, with the stakes being your reputation and my happiness.

To play the game, I allowed you to win my heart. You acquitted yourself of your task with verve, convincing me of your genuine love, while remaining open and honest throughout. You made no promise that I might find cause to call broken, and upon your departure what sorrow I felt arose entirely from minor expectations I had formed despite myself and despite your pellucid representation of the circumstances. As long as these lasted, I was able to give myself over fully to pleasure without loss of clear sight. As a result, I must confess to having enjoyed our affair and having emerged from it none the worse. You can thus rightly account this engagement a glorious victory, upon which you have not only my congratulations but my thanks, as I have benefited no less than you by your dexterity. I must accordingly concede the utter failure of my plan to adduce the example of myself in meeting the second part of our challenge; namely, that I produce someone who has suffered for having loved you.

That is not to concede that such a person does not exist.

It was an unhappy circumstance by which that very woman crossed my path some years ago. I met her through several ladies who had drawn me into small acts of charity on behalf of our poor, of whom there are far too many in the city. I noticed her face as I was doling out bread and secondhand clothes. In time, she grew less shy. I won her confidence, and she came to recount to me her sad history. So different was it from your own report—and not only because she called you by your Christian name—that it took a long time for me to realize that my Jacques was her Giacomo and that the unhappy child could only be your Lucia.

She is the guarantor of victory I have been harboring since we first struck our wager. In the fact of her existence, therefore, I win, though if I am honest I count myself a loser as well, for having grown so fond of you, I would have rather left you without damaging your unquestioning faith in your own beneficence. For doing otherwise I am sorry.

Should we never meet again, then, have no fear. What happened between us was a game that has been played with mutual satisfaction. You can therefore record a substantial credit beside my name in your ledger, a credit that I trust will cancel the deficit of happiness of her whose existence I have regrettably been obliged to disclose.

Farewell!

Oh, yes, if you would like to see her misery with your own eyes, Lucia can be found on Friday and Saturday evenings in one of the gaming houses on the Zeedijk. I beg you to study her first from a distance. She is not a pretty sight. Whether you choose to approach her or not, I leave to the disposition of your

emotions, which I have come to trust. In this, I pray you will be
governed by the love you once felt, refusing judgment on a life
you have not lived yourself. And be prepared for the worst.
   May love be ever with you,

                                    Your Galathée de Pompignac

I completed this letter toward morning and had it delivered
at the earliest opportunity. The rest of the day I tried to rest. It
was bitter cold. For hours I lay in bed, listening to the silence of
the frost that overlay the city like a coverlet, muffling all voices.
This kept me calm. Toward evening I put on a patched dress I
had bought with particular purpose at the rag market. It was
tattered and torn; I hadn't worn anything like it for years. I
adorned it in no way but for my grandfather's pendant, which I
wore clearly visible around my neck. Finally, at the door, I took
off my veil.

   I walked to the dike and chose the Gulf of Guinea. It wasn't
the worst of the establishments there, though still far from salu-
brious. Not knowing how long I would have to wait, I took a
chair close to the fire. Catching the full glow of the flames there
I stood out in the room, which was otherwise quite gloomy.

   People were dancing. The regular girls were surprised to see
me and had questions, but after a while the novelty dissolved
and one by one they climbed the stairs with clients in tow. Only
one complained that my face was scaring people off and ruining
it for the rest of them. I responded by grabbing the poker from
the hearth and brandishing it like a loon, whereupon she fled.
The landlady brought a tankard of beer to calm me. I sat there
and waited, slowly growing drowsy in the heat.

MY IMPERFECTION. This was the part of my plan I had shrunk
from the most: having to lay it bare once again. But to this point,

the act had not proved so painful. On the contrary, it had been hidden away for so long that the feelings that caused me to hide it were not easily revived. It would be ridiculous to say that I suddenly derived some kind of pride from my appearance, but at that moment it wasn't a source of shame either. And although I searched for it, as one might a beacon that has unexpectedly been moved, I couldn't find the grief I had always taken for granted. What had changed about me? I felt stronger, knowing I would love despite everything; the certainty of that was already growing within me. It was the words for it that had not yet come to me. For I couldn't fathom how this inner metamorphosis could have transformed my sentiments about my appearance.

My eyes drifted down to the flames licking at the wood. The flickering encouraged my thoughts to wander even more. And suddenly the drowning man was before me again, the one who almost went under, holding so tight he couldn't be saved until he let go. Two or three vicious sparks shot up out of the hearth in that same instant and, together with the log being consumed by the flames, my thoughts burst open. Suddenly I saw, like some saintly vision, the lesson Fate had been trying to teach me.

FOR TOO MANY YEARS, I confused love with desire. As a girl, I had seen people yearning. Some went out to hunt for love; others stayed home, restlessly waiting for someone to come and offer it to them. People talked about it as if life itself depended upon it. Those without it needed to find it, and the sooner the better. Those who had enjoyed but lost it had no more urgent need than to replace it, if necessary by stealing the treasure someone else had laid away. To acquire wealth or fame was child's play compared with acquiring love. Even having a chunk of bread was less important, because love was well known to extinguish hunger. Lovers, I had thought, could withstand every deprivation for the sake of winning the prize they had set their hearts on. And no one was more praiseworthy than one who would lay down his life to win the love of another.

And yet, for all the effort applied to its attainment, love was plainly something enjoyed only by a lucky few. All others were pitiable and self-pitying. I had known some to set their sights on one who would not love them in return, even while rejecting as undesirable another love offered to them freely. The unrequited were not infrequently driven by misery to renounce their original passion and seek one they had formerly despised, only to discover it now beyond reach. Those who refused to elect someone novel were just as susceptible to unhappiness. They were the ones who waited for love to find them and, at first sight of its approach, threw the door open and ran out to meet it, taking up a position by the side of the road with their arms outstretched to embrace the long-awaited gift. There followed utter bafflement when the nearly beloved turned and fled, terrified by so much ardor. After years of unanswered longing, they fell into melancholy, finally losing even the love they felt for themselves.

All these people, without exception, thought that love was their right, and none understood, except on rare fleeting occasions, why they could never obtain it.

Before I knew Giacomo, I had not known the treasure that so many around me sought. It was infinite joy to be given his love and to have known while I had it that it was mine. For years after he had left, taking it with him, I cherished the memory, even as I could perceive that too slipping away. Still, like a little girl walking on the beach with a heap of sand in her fist, I was as proud of what I had saved as I was saddened by the memory of what had slipped through my fingers.

In the end, I would recite the few things I could remember like an incantation to summon again that short moment of happiness. To recall the words and the scenes in which Giacomo had given me his love assumed a sacramental power. And in his absence, by some mystery, I could put myself in his place and my own in turn: in one instant imagining myself Giacomo, whispering endearments in Lucia's ear; in the next, Lucia whispering her faithful assent into his. Perhaps it was the endless repetition that cast a spell on me—the same words, the same gestures, imagined over and over—as a scientist might peer without end at some bit of creation, desperate to divine a pattern. In any case, suddenly, in the grip of this trance, an astonishing thought occurred to me. It was so simple that at first I mistrusted it.

During one morning lesson, I remember, Pompignac had shown me the frontispiece of the *Encyclopedia*, where Diderot placed an engraving: Reason and Emotion together pulling the veil away from Truth. Truth now stood before me no less naked and incontrovertible. Was it possible that, without realizing it, most of us have the power to create our own happiness? That we can find certain things only once we abandon the search for them?

All my most indelibly happy memories were linked to moments in which I had expressed my love for Giacomo. It's not that I felt less elated when the young abbé showed his love for me—far from it—but then my happiness was made of gratitude. There was between this giving and receiving only a shade of difference, negligible and almost imperceptible, during our courtship. I might never have noticed it had fate not separated us so soon.

If, as I had first come to believe, the blessing of love is in receiving and keeping it, my happiness should have vanished once I no longer had Giacomo to love me. And yet it was not so. I knew my deepest happiness *without* Giacomo, when he was in Venice and I, disfigured, was recovering from my illness. There can be no mistake about that. I was never so full of love's happiness as in that moment when, with him far away, I resolved to sacrifice for his sake the life that was to have been mine. The blessing of my love was not in being loved but loving!

Now that I understood this, after all these years, I found myself holding the one weapon that can withstand any attack. It is the deeper truth that lies behind the visible, just as the eyes of Santa Lucia are engraved on the back of the glass of my pendant and become visible only when struck by a certain light.

Everything comes down to this: the reason for every word I have written and every word I will write. I am recounting my life for you so that you may know this secret without the pain of discovering it: We are unhappy because we think that love is something we require from someone else. Our salvation depends on a simple gesture that is nonetheless the most difficult act we can perform: We must give away the thing we most long for. Not to *receive* but to *give*.

So do we conjure triumph from defeat. This is the lesson of the life forced upon me by my imperfection.

UNMASKED, HYPNOTIZED by the fire, calmed by my tankard of beer, I let my thoughts wander a little longer. If I had been like other girls, I might have spent my whole life without giving my happiness a second thought. But in the darkness through which I had been forced to roam, I saw a glimmer of this truth. *This is my salvation,* I thought, *and I owe it to this face of mine.* There was in that moment a grandeur in my affliction that reason could never have contrived.

You see a matriarch's wisdom in her wrinkles, a general's courage in his wounds. There is no proper claim to distinction but the things that have marked us.

"YOU SHOULD HAVE LISTENED when I told you, Seingalt." In the beat of a heart, that cry put me on the alert. It was Rijgerbos. He was standing in the doorway, ready to turn his back on the stinking room with the first glance. "The only thing we'll find in here is a dose of the clap."

Giacomo paid him no mind and stepped within.

"You can be mighty stubborn," Rijgerbos grumbled in his best French, following his friend as if wading through a manure pile, taking great care not to touch anyone or anything. "I don't know who could have recommended this place for your entertainment, but, blast him, he's no lover of cleanliness!"

They sat down and ordered a drink. Meanwhile, Giacomo peered out across the dimly lit room. Twice his eyes came to rest on me. In both instances the gaze was paralyzing, but it didn't occur to him that I could be the woman he was searching for, and he twice looked away with no sign of recognition. Finally I stood and approached him. Those few yards were the unimaginable bridge over an abyss I had resolved never to cross. I laid a hand on his shoulder. He brushed it away with annoyance, scarcely looking toward me. It was only after he understood I would not retreat from him that he stood to look at me more closely. My face. My throat. My whole body. My breast with the pendant he knew at once from long ago. Then my face again, his face transforming from fierceness to disbelief. His pain was no less severe than my own. With his eyes instantly full of tears, he turned his head to hide his revulsion but couldn't turn away from me completely. Instead, to conceal his disquiet, he grabbed his glass, draining it in a single gulp. He sniffed and dabbed his face. Only then did he turn back to me. I affected simple happiness at seeing him again. He managed a smile when I told him that the years had changed him so I hardly recognized him.

"I am as happy to see you prosperous," I said in Italian, attempting the higher, softer voice of my youth, "as you must be disturbed at seeing what has become of me."

"Lucia," he said finally. "But I had no idea. . . ."

"You *were* told that you could find me here?"

"Of course," he stuttered, "I would not have come to such a place but . . . but for you." Slowly he regained his composure. "After all—" Without taking his eyes off me for a moment, he took me by the shoulders and studied me as if trying to rediscover some vestige of his former affection. Finally he could only say, "After all, I loved you!"

To the horror of Rijgerbos, who didn't understand a word of Italian and had stood there gaping at his friend's intimacies with this wretched creature, Giacomo proposed that we rent a room upstairs for an hour so I could sit down and tell them what had become of me.

I REMAINED TRUE to the lie I had conceived in Pasiano, the story I had directed my mother to tell Giacomo, and embellished it with a few artful details. That L'Aigle had seduced me. That though I had determined to stay faithful, I was slow to resist his advance, allowing him some playful encouragement until he would not be deterred. That I'd wanted to kill myself when I realized that I bore his child but, being unable to undertake this violence, had chosen instead to flee the scandal. That I had taken to the streets and that my body had been ravaged by love. Giacomo stared at me with glassy eyes. My appearance had shocked him so it scarcely mattered what I was saying. Suddenly, he interrupted me and began to wail self-reproach, confessing his guilt in my suffering.

It was not what I had intended by this fabulation. I had hoped to erase in one stroke both my guilt and his own. Refusing his pleas for forgiveness, I told him that what had happened could only be put down to Fate. Now that he knew, I suggested that he could perhaps find it in himself to understand me, at least somewhat, and then, without spite, be able to forget me.

Rijgerbos, still plainly baffled at the goings-on, didn't dare to look up. He hid behind a newspaper and rang for more wine.

"If I had returned to Pasiano sooner, as I could easily have done—how differently it would have all turned out!"

"And if I had been truly worthy of your love," I countered, "I would not have allowed myself to be seduced." I was growing weary of his confessions of guilt. I had contrived this meeting to extinguish any remaining feeling for me, not to fan the embers of his pity. "I loved you," I said as coldly as I could, "but obviously not well enough to flee from L'Aigle."

"If you had never met me, if I hadn't stirred your passions, your heart would have still been pure when L'Aigle approached you. And his seduction would have been fruitless. If I had not held you in such regard, if I had loved you less well and satisfied your desires rather than arousing them chastely, I would not have left you languishing and frustrated and so subject to that villain's temptation."

"It is of no matter now," I said coolly. I feared the power of these emotions and was at pains to remain unmoved by them. But my spirits sank. The sadness in his eyes reduced me almost to tears, the flow of which I was able to stem only by the grace of what he said next.

"God, I was such a fool!" Giacomo lamented. "Priding myself on preserving your virtue. What a shameful fool! As if some divinity had appointed this day to remind me of what I have known since my wretched return to Pasiano: It is unpardonable sin not to take what love puts before you."

In a flash, his tone brought our positions back into focus. Here in so few words was the wisdom of his life. The star he had followed led along a path that had diverged farther and farther from my own. I could feel only sorrow at the impossibility of ever leading him back to the point where our ways had once crossed.

I told the gentlemen I would take my leave of them. I proposed to lead them to Giovanna and Danaë, who would be pleased to amuse them for the rest of the night. They acceded to the idea passively, by not refusing. We said our farewells at the girls' door. I was less surprised by Giacomo's tears than by my own indifference, as if upon them I was floating away from him.

Now I let go and was delivered.

Walking away, I heard Rijgerbos snort with relief, at seeing the end of the whole puzzling interlude and at the prospect of what might yet become an evening of genuine pleasure.

7

THE SEA IS CALM. We are in the third week of the voyage. I have just now been on deck. I take great pleasure in our sailing straight for the setting sun. Against the volcanic colors of the sky, the sails look as if they're on fire. Another thing I enjoy: going to the bow and leaning out as far as I can over the railing. Suspended above the waves that way, I am able to imagine us, for a moment, going our solitary way together. I have no regrets. This fate is unalterable like that of a coin cast overboard in the middle of the ocean. No matter how desperately I might later need it, it will have sunk to the bottom, never to be retrieved no matter what I might do. That comforts me. What I have lost is beyond my reach forever. I have no choice but to forget it. The future is not different from the past in this respect; there is nothing to be done about it but to be on our way.

When dark has fallen, I return to my cabin and continue the story I am writing in the hope that you will one day read it.

NO SOONER HAD I LEFT Giacomo, even before I had quit the alley, than I felt myself violently sick, as if having taken one of the ghastly emetics Fra Onofrio had given me as a child, when I had foolishly swallowed the leaves of a poisonous shrub. As it was then, the purgation now was violent and deep-seated and came without warning, over and over, all the way home without respite. I spent the rest of that night in bed shivering, unsure of the cause of my convulsions, which were too powerful to put down to spoiled food. In the morning Jamieson came by. He had arranged his passage and would be departing as soon as the winds were favorable. I began to wish him a safe voyage, but he interrupted me, and was in such an agitation that I concluded he had come to say more than goodbye.

"I don't know how you are getting on with that Frenchman," he said. "It's clear enough that when he's in town, my goose is cooked. Try though I might to present myself as handsome and witty, you are not to be found in this world, but off in some other place, where I'm as invisible as an Indian in a poppy field."

"Shame on you!" I laughed. "If I didn't know better, I might think you jealous!"

"Jealousy," grumbled Jamieson. "Another French vice! Wouldn't exist at all except for all those tight ruffles constricting their blood. That's not it, girl, hear me please. I wasn't planning on mentioning it. It's just . . . I like to see you happy."

I thanked him for all the pleasant evenings we had shared and the kindnesses he had shown me. I began to recall one such occasion, but he wasn't to be distracted.

"It may surprise you, but I know your nature. You're not hard to hurt. I've seen it with my own eyes!" For a moment, neither of us spoke; I recalled the instant he discovered my secret, which moment he must surely have had in mind. "Who's going to be here to watch over you, damn it? That's all I want to know. And apart from that"—he no longer dared to look at me but began studying his fingers, picking at a nail—"I do have a tender spot for women, you know that."

"And we are all very glad of it."

"No jokes. I've been around. And I am not blind; I can see

your breasts swelling up. Will you tell me you are not carrying a child?"

"If I were, it could not possibly be yours."

"No," he snapped, "I know that. But the French being, as everyone knows, a good deal less concerned with hygiene—"

"What is your implication, Mr. Jamieson?"

"I heard that chevalier of yours myself, boasting at the tavern that a Frenchman would sooner tie a lemon pressed dry to the end of his member than suffer wearing those sheep's guts the madams of Amsterdam force on their clients."

"It is no business of yours and of no interest to me, Mr. Jamieson," I said brusquely, standing up to say that our conversation was over. I was saddened to think that our friendship was to end this way, but seeing that his coarseness had already assured it would not be otherwise, he continued pigheadedly to badger me as I led him to the door.

"Let me say it plain and once only: I know you and I— I might just as well say it, what do I care?—I'll take you as you are, past and all, that's what I mean to say. I don't expect love. These hands have done so much tanning that they're too hard for love. They will never become finely manicured Parisian fingertips. No, I might be able to use them to scrub a hide until it gleams perfect and smooth, but for caressing a woman as she would like, they will not do. I can, however, promise that the rough work will be theirs alone, and your lot will be as a lady's without worry of the past or for the future."

Before he could continue his lunatic declarations, I slammed the door on him, but even from the street he kept raving.

"A lemon, d'you hear me? Of all the citrus fruits, he chose the lemon and not the orange. Ha! That's the glory of France in a nutshell!" After this he fell silent. When I concluded he had departed, there was another knock at the door, this one very respectful and restrained. I did not answer it, but soon I heard

Jamieson's voice, now tame and childlike. "I just wanted to say that I can't bear to leave you here without protection from the worst of it."

I CAN'T BE SURE who your father is. It could be *he*, though it might just as likely be another. For me it makes little difference. I shall love you as I have never loved anyone, having only lately understood the sentiment in its true sense. I will teach its meaning to you at every opportunity, and when you're old enough, you will read these words by which I aim to explain your mother's insistence on this one thing: love! That might not seem much, but I learned it—you know that now—against the odds. In that sense you are certainly the child of Lucia and Giacomo. Don't judge them too harshly; were it not for their love, you would not have mine.

JAMIESON HAD APPARENTLY given up when another knock, this one quite urgent, was heard at the door. The courier expressed great relief at finding me at home, having been charged to deliver his letter at all cost, following me if necessary to Utrecht, Cologne, or even farther east. The envelope was weighty. When I opened it, banknotes fell out.

Chère Galathée,

Enclosed please find the sum of 200 ecus as settlement of our wager. You have earned it fairly, although I would gladly have given ten—no, one hundred times as much to have been spared last night's discovery.

Lucia was indeed to be found in the area to which you directed me. When she approached, I turned away, but it was too late. She had recognized me and began to address me in dismal tones. Her looks were indescribable. She cannot be more than thirty but gives the impression of being fifty years old or more, and of course for all purposes a woman is always as old as she looks. This superannuated aspect I gathered to be the result of a gross debauchery to which she had dedicated herself since I last saw her in Pasiano. A courier had impregnated her and taken her to lie in at Trieste, where he lived off her for some five or six months before abandoning her. But you are doubtless more completely acquainted with her wretched history. She drained two bottles in the hour it took her to relate it. She spoke most highly of you, and I beg you to continue to show her your kindness. She has no one else. I slipped her a few ducats, but if, upon your return to Amsterdam, you could find it in your heart to grant the piteous thing a few more mercies, I would be eternally in your debt. Finally, she led us to two girls who work for her, paying her half of everything they earn. As her beauty has disappeared, she has no alternative. It is the classic ending.

Though her ruin happened without my knowledge, I cannot deny a most profound feeling of guilt. This puts the disposition of our wager beyond question. Poor Lucia, she has become not merely ugly but something far worse: repulsive! How heartrending to see what we once loved trampled underfoot.

Rest assured, chère Galathée, of the ardor with which I await your return and our reunion,

I am, faithfully,
Seingalt

That same afternoon the wind changed direction with some suddenness. I reached the logical conclusion that, having tried my luck north and south, it was now time to go west. I took a few dresses and packed them in a case, secreting among them what jewelry I had left. Mindful of all the unsavory characters around the harbor, I carried Seingalt's banknotes under my clothes. I gathered up what was left of my half ream and on those sheets have now recounted my history for you, which I would vouchsafe to no soul but one who would love me without condition. I was at the quay at half past one, not a moment too soon, as the captain wished to be at sea by nightfall. With the 200 ecus, I paid my passage rather than oblige myself to Mr. Jamieson. When he saw me walking up the gangplank, that big clumsy man was overcome with joy and cried like a baby. No matter what course my relations with him take, I know he will be a father to you, for he has given me his word you shall want for nothing.

New York, he says, is now grand and elegant, nothing like Amsterdam. There are some three thousand redbrick mansions along its jumbled streets, which are wide and paved and lined on either side with curbs for walking. There is no place in Europe that can compare. The city is surrounded by water and by broad docks with great warehouses, two of which are owned wholly by Jamieson, one for tobacco and one for skins.

Today we sighted land, probably Virginia, which means we are at most but two days from New York.

We have made it to the other side.

The coast looks charming, but it seems that life outside the cities is hard. The people in this part of the world are rough but marked, so it is said, by an unreasonable optimism. As if there were any other kind! According to Jamieson, adversity only hardens their determination to succeed. I like that, swimming against the current. America still has few scars.

Perhaps this is what compels me to part from Europe. That land is too old. It has been wounded too many times, the earth plowed too often and too deeply. It has been cruelly awakened too often ever again to drift off into careless dreams. Time and again, the Europeans have learned that following their natures leads only to chaos, and they no longer dare to trust their inclinations. Instead they have delivered themselves up to the savior of reason. They answer their fear of the incomprehensible by trying to lay every last secret bare. Giacomo is that way, going so far as to wish to rationalize his happiness. This you must forgive him. One can never completely escape the confusion of one's age, and I am no exception. For a long time, I too tried to carry the yoke of reason, but it was too heavy for me. I rejected it. Someone in my place can ill afford to see things as they are. For you it will be different; born of both, the old and the new, heart and mind, you will be free to choose between them.

I have let go.

I did not go under.

Author's Postscript

LUCY JAMIESON was buried on February 11, 1802, in the church-yard of St. Paul's in Flatbush, New York. According to the head-stone, she survived her husband by more than thirty years. Three children were born during their marriage. The oldest was a son. She named him Jacob.

Giacomo Casanova never discovered the full truth of Lucia's life and suffering. Nonetheless, he describes her in his memoirs as the first of a mere two women he ever wronged. Despite this, he dedicates only a few pages to this great love. First he recounts their meeting, his feelings, and her betrayal in Pasiano. Later he describes the shock of encountering her again in an Amsterdam brothel, where she had become not just ugly, *but something worse: repulsive.* He seems almost uninterested in how she came to be there or why she gave up her earlier happiness.

Besides the books and archives I used to reconstruct Lucia's story, Casanova's own words were crucial. Like many brilliant people, he has room for different truths in his memory. In his description of his adventures in Holland, where he traveled under the name Seingalt, these truths sometimes clash, just as they do elsewhere in his *Histoire de ma vie.* Names, places, times, and even years can differ from the apparent facts. This could be deliberate, to make the story more readable or to disguise the truth, but it could also be put down to the tendency of memory to reorder and reshape events. Giacomo often combines different visits into one or divides a particular event into several parts. From all these truths I have chosen the one most consistent with Lucia's story. In particular I took Casanova's account as the basis for his conversations with Lucia in Pasiano. The dialogue is sometimes identical, though in my version it is always described from Lucia's perspective. From his memoirs I have also adopted a number of ideas and anecdotes that shed light on Casanova's character and the customs of the day.* Other books that proved instructive include Dr. D. Hoek's *Casanova in Holland* and J. Rives Childs's *Casanova*.

The life and entourage of Anna Morandi Manzolini have been described by Angela Ghirardi of the University of Bologna. In that same city, Anna's wax self-portrait has been preserved—together with some of her anatomical models—in the Museo di Anatomia Umana Normale. Marcello Venuti himself wrote about the excavations that he and his brothers carried out near Herculaneum. Zélide's flying machines are the lifework of Charles Dellschau. The drawings I describe can be found in the Menil Collection in Houston, Texas, along with the secret recipe for *soupe*.

I gained most of my knowledge of the customs and practice of prostitution in Lucia's day from Lotte van de Pol's magnificent study *The Whores of Amsterdam* and also derived some terms from a 1681 book with the same title, a detailed account of an excursion to the city's brothels and gaming houses. The classification of whores as horses comes from the mid-eighteenth-

*Translator's note: The author cites Theo Kars's Dutch translation. For this English version, I referred to several Casanova translations, in particular the complete translation by Willard Trask (*History of My Life*, Harcourt Brace, 1966) and the selection from Casanova's works translated by Stephen Sartarelli and Sophie Hawkes (*The Story of My Life*, Penguin Classics, 2001).

century book *The True Story of Fleeced Farmer Gys*. Once again I was greatly helped by the discussions film director Ineke Smits and I had with prostitutes while researching our film *Whore's Sermon*. I am indebted to these women for the trust they showed by telling us about their motives and experiences, their emotions, and their dreams. I am grateful to the Dutch prostitutes' collective The Red Thread for establishing our contact with them. When reconstructing Lucia's sessions in the anatomical theater and for an impression of the state of anatomy in the eighteenth century, I was greatly aided by Annet Mooij's *Doctors of Amsterdam: Patient Care, Medical Training, and Research (1650– 2000)*.

Harlequin Hulla, the play Galathée goes to see with Casanova, was written in 1747 by Jacques Japin.

A NOTE ON THE TYPE

THIS BOOK was set in Monotype Dante, a typeface designed by Giovanni Mardersteig (1892–1977). Conceived as a private type for the Officina Bodoni in Verona, Italy, Dante was originally cut only for hand composition by Charles Malin, the famous Parisian punch cutter, between 1946 and 1952. Its first use was in an edition of Boccaccio's *Trattatello in laude di Dante* that appeared in 1954. The Monotype Corporation's version of Dante followed in 1957. Although modeled on the Aldine type used for Pietro Cardinal Bembo's treatise *De Aetna* in 1945, Dante is a thoroughly modern interpretation of the venerable face.

Composed by Stratford Publishing Services,
Brattleboro, Vermont
Printed and bound by R.R. Donnelley & Sons,
Harrisonburg, Virginia
Designed by Virginia Tan